For all the readers who love holiday romances just as much as I do.

Be merry. Be bright. And read long into the night!

A holiday romance with a dash of romantic suspense and a former military hero who is so not feeling the festive spirit...

Bah humbug. Bounty hunter Jake Hale hates Christmas. He doesn't do twinkling lights, festive packages, and you definitely won't ever catch him singing Christmas carols. What he will do? Track down the worst of the scum out there. The former special ops soldier makes merry by tossing the naughty into prison cells and getting a grand pay day. Ho, ho, ho.

Then a ghost from Christmas past walks through his door.

True Blakely is always at the top of the nice list. Beautiful, sweet, with an innocence that—yep, he might have been tempted to destroy once or twice—she's there to hire him. There have been a string of dangerous accidents in her life, and True fears that someone is trying to kill her. Not at all the sort of case that Jake would usually take—he hunts down the criminals *after* they jump bail, not before they've even been arrested. But one look into True's bedroom eyes, and he can't refuse. Maybe he still is a bit too tempted by the girl who got away...and surely one nice act won't kill him? For her, he can play the hero.

He'll close the case and be home in time for Christmas dinner.

Except, on the first morning of his investigation, he finds a dead body. One waiting underneath True's glittering Christmas tree. The attacks are real, and it's clear that someone is gunning for True. But Jake is on the job now, and no one is going to hurt her. His protective instincts are in overdrive...and so is the desperate desire that he's always felt for True. This time, he's done fighting that desire. He'll finally show True just how fantastic it can be when you aren't nice. Welcome to his naughty list.

HOLDING OUT FOR A HOLIDAY HERO is a hot Christmas romance with action, laughter, thrills, and enough steam to melt the Christmas snow. Opposites attract? Check. Super alpha hero? Check. Danger, desire? Double check. Santa isn't the only one checking things off his list...Jake Hale is taking care of business, too, and this unlikely hero is about to fall hard and fast for the woman of his Christmas dreams.

Holding Out For A Holiday Hero

A Ho-Ho-Hot Holiday Romance

Cynthia Eden

Published by Hocus Pocus Publishing, Inc.

If you have any problems, comments, or questions about this publication, please contact info@hocuspocuspublishing.com.

Chapter One

"Sleigh bells ring, are you listening?"

"No, I'm fucking not. Stop ringing them." – *Jake Hale*

THE GHOST OF CHRISTMAS PAST HAD JUST WALKED her sexy self into his office.

Jake Hale blinked—then blinked again—because he was pretty sure that he might be hallucinating. Or dreaming. Yeah, this could be a dream. A really hot fantasy because surely there was no way that True Blakely had just walked her gorgeous ass into his bounty hunting office.

A soft glow came and went behind her body, and Christmas music seemed to drift in the air around her. She wore a form-fitting, red dress, one that displayed all of her glorious curves to true perfection. Her dark, nearly black hair tumbled over her shoulders, and he could see a few white snowflakes in the thick mass. Her blue eyes—the most unforgettable, brightest shade of blue imaginable—locked on him.

Now, if this was truly one of his fantasies, she'd open those lush, red lips of hers and say something like... *"Jake, I need you."*

Then they would spend the night doing all sorts of incredibly unspeakable things to each other. The kind of things that would have her clawing her nails down his back and screaming his name while she came for him.

In the doorway, the Ghost of Christmas Past parted her lush, red lips and murmured, "Jake? Jake Hale?" Her husky voice seemed to wrap around him.

He'd been reclining in his desk chair, with his scuffed sneakers propped on the edge of his desk.

"Jake, I need you," she said.

Holy hell. This holiday season had just gotten *way* brighter. He swung his sneakers to the floor and jumped to his feet. His chair rolled behind him with a screech of its wheels.

Jake stared at True. Best dream ever. And then he—

"Hey, boss!" His assistant Perry Cornwell poked his head beside True's. "The lady insisted on seeing you. I told her that we were closing up for the night, but she said you two were old friends."

Perry would never be in any dream he had. Jake glowered at the kid. Perry was twenty-two, as of last week. The kid had been hounding Jake forever for a job, and he'd given in—reluctantly—about two months ago. And now he had an assistant who'd insisted on putting up a damn tree in their small lobby. A lop-sided, Charlie Brown look-alike Christmas tree.

That was where the glow came from. The faint flicker of lights that he could see behind True? That was coming from the sad Christmas tree. And Perry was playing his annoying, holly jolly music again. How many times had Jake asked him to kill the holiday songs?

But he pulled his glare from Perry and focused on what mattered. A most unlikely Ghost of Christmas Past. One who should not be in his office.

True stared straight at Jake with her big, gorgeous eyes. She wet her lips. *Sweet heaven.* "We...*are* friends, right, Jake?"

Uh, no. They were not. But, wow, that voice of hers was sexy. It seemed to stroke right over him.

"You remember me?" she asked, with a faint hitch in her breathing.

Not like he could forget her. She'd pretty much starred in every single teenage dream that he'd had. Not that the upright and uptight True had ever known that fact. She'd been the homecoming queen. He'd been the one voted most likely to cause extreme havoc.

Jake had been thrilled with that particular award.

If True only knew all of the things he'd always wanted to do with her...

"I need you," she told him again.

No dream. But also no sex-fueled declaration from her. The woman actually sounded desperate. Maybe even a little afraid.

And Jake realized he hadn't spoken a word to her. *Old habits died hard.* Back in the day, he'd always gotten tongue-tied around her. So he'd stared and glowered and probably scared her to death. He definitely could not have left a positive impression on her.

So why is True here, asking for my help?

"Uh, boss?" Perry edged closer. The Santa hat on his head bobbed.

Seriously, a Santa hat? They ran a bounty hunting office. They weren't supposed to be cute. They were supposed to be scary.

"You, ah, you gonna help your old friend?" Perry's expression clearly said they should help the woman in distress.

"Got her," Jake growled.

True flinched.

Hell. Jake cleared his throat. He could do way better than this. He wasn't some punk kid any longer. He'd traveled the whole world. He'd fought for his country. Seen and done things that would give most people nightmares.

A five-foot-five woman with bedroom eyes should not have him quivering in his sneakers.

I'm not quivering. I am turned on. Just like in the old days. He'd seen True, and, bam, instant arousal. "I'll talk to my...friend." Interesting word. Not one that he'd ever associated with her. "You go on home, Perry."

But Perry lingered. "You sure, boss? I'm happy to help." His brown eyes swept toward True and lingered a little too long.

"*I'm sure.*"

Perry jumped.

So maybe Jake's words had held a bit of bite. That was just who he was. Jake waved toward his assistant. A wave—maybe a shooing motion. Whatever. "Turn off the Christmas lights on your way out, would you? And kill the damn music."

Perry pouted.

Really? A pout? Assistants did not pout.

"Kill. It." An order.

"Consider it killed." Perry glanced adoringly at True. "Very nice to meet you."

"You, too." A weak smile. One that never reached her eyes. Now, that was odd. Because in the past, True had always been quick to flash a megawatt smile. Her bright smile had been the first thing he noticed about her. And why in the hell was he obsessing over her smile?

Get your shit together, man. You are not some idiot with a crush. Those days are long gone.

Perry exited.

True stepped fully into Jake's office, she shut the door behind her, and the music died. Thankfully. Jake was so not in the mood for hearing about people dashing through the snow. He personally hated the white, fluffy crap, and unfortunately, the town of Rosewood, Georgia—about eighty miles north of Atlanta—had just gotten hit with a batch of snow.

Most people were thrilled. Chatting about having a white Christmas.

Jake just thought the snow was a pain in the ass.

True stood there, twisting her hands in front of her body, and biting her delectable lower lip. He waited for her to say something. To explain exactly why she was in his office. But the moments just ticked by in silence. Curious now, he moved to the front of his desk. He propped a hip on the wooden edge and motioned to the chair near him. "Why don't you have a seat?"

Her black boots slid across the floor before she tentatively lowered into the chair. Her eyes never left his face.

Automatically, he rubbed a hand over his jaw and felt the scrape of stubble. Great. He probably looked like hell. He'd chased down two bounties that day—rough catches. His clothes were battered, his hair disheveled, and he *might* have still been sporting the remains of a black eye. Clearly, he was no Prince Charming. But she'd been the one to seek *him* out. Curiosity was about to kill him. "Why are you here?" he asked her.

"I...need to hire you."

Jake laughed.

She didn't. "You...do remember me? I mean, I know we didn't exactly run in the same circles back in school."

He snorted.

Her eyes narrowed. "Sorry I wasn't *cool* enough for you."

Wait. Hold up. The homecoming queen had just said that she wasn't cool enough for *him?*

"But we had two classes together," she continued determinedly. "You sat behind me in both of them."

He'd picked those seats deliberately. True had always smelled like strawberries. By sitting behind her, he'd been able to savor that sweet scent.

"You *must* remember me—"

"I remember you."

Her shoulders sagged. "I'm desperate."

The people who came to him usually were. Thoroughly intrigued now, he studied her with a more assessing gaze. "You want me to hunt someone for you." That was his bread and butter, after all. *Bounty hunting*. While working special ops, he'd become one fine hunter. These days, he stayed stateside, but he still hunted down the perps who thought they were going to escape justice.

No one escaped on his watch.

"Yes." A sigh. "That's exactly what I want you to do."

Now they were working in his wheelhouse. Jake nodded. "Well, tell me the perp's name, and I'll start to dig. If he's jumped bail, then I should be able to—"

She was shaking her head. No.

"No...what?" Jake asked. His nostrils flared. He thought he'd just caught the scent of strawberries. Still as mouth-watering as ever. *Do not drool on the potential client.* That would be bad form.

"I...don't have a name." Halting.

His eyes narrowed on her. "That will make things more challenging."

She glanced away from him. "Please don't think I'm crazy."

"Uh, okay."

Her stare flickered back to him and lingered. "Someone is trying to kill me."

Jake leapt away from the desk. "*What?*" He grabbed the arms of her chair and leaned in toward her. "Who the hell is doing that?"

"I don't know, exactly."

His hands tightened on the chair arms. "Have you gone to the police?"

"Yes, but they didn't believe me."

And why not?

"They think I'm imagining things. *I'm not.*" She was adamant. "Someone shoved me off the sidewalk a few days ago. I was almost hit by a car, but, luckily, the driver swerved at the last moment. I got away with some scrapes and bruises."

He caught her hands in his. Electricity seemed to pulse through him as he touched her. *Damn.* Gritting his teeth, Jake turned over her hands. He immediately noticed two things. First, her skin was insanely soft. But, second, he could see the healing scrapes on her palms.

She must have slammed down her hands to try and break her fall.

"I came back to town last year. After my divorce."

Right. He knew that she'd been married to a lawyer in Atlanta.

"I've been working at the museum in town, and two nights ago, part of our Egyptian exhibit came tumbling down toward me. That exhibit piece was secure, I swear it was, and I barely jumped out of the way in time. If I hadn't looked up when I did, if I hadn't heard a faint scratch of sound that alerted me, I could have been knocked out. Or worse."

Damn.

"And...there's more."

He maintained his position. And, yes, indeed, he did smell strawberries. And maybe his thumbs were lightly rubbing along the inside of her palms.

"I could swear someone has been in my house. Things have been moved around in my den and bedroom. I can feel someone watching me. I-I don't think I'm safe in my own home." Tears gleamed in her eyes.

He whipped back and dropped her hands, as if he'd been burned.

Jake had never understood how to handle a woman's tears. Truth be told, a woman's tears horrified him. He took two quick steps away from her.

She blinked quickly and only a single teardrop slid down her cheek. True immediately wiped it away. "The cops said...they were just accidents. Accidents happen. That I was jumping to conclusions."

"And what about your house?" Jake sawed a hand over his jaw again.

One shoulder rolled in a shrug. "They didn't come look at my house. I was told they are short staffed and only come out for *real* crimes." She peered directly into his eyes. "This is real. I know it. Someone is trying to hurt me."

The hell someone would hurt her. *Not on my watch.* Except, he wasn't on watch. But—

"That's why I want to hire you." She gave a determined nod. Her hair slid over her shoulders. "You can find him."

"Uh..." There seemed to be some confusion. "I hunt criminals *after* they've been arrested. Typically, that would be when they are trying to jump bail and escape town." And he tracked them down with absolute determination.

She rose. Edged closer to him.

He stiffened.

She was just inches away from him. Touchably close.

"Everyone talks about you in this town," True admitted.

People needed to mind their own business.

"They say that you came home with a fistful of medals."

He'd also come home with plenty of bullet wounds and a few scars from knife attacks. Did people talk about his injuries as much as they talked about his medals? Probably not.

"You fought and you served your country, and then you opened this business. And since opening it, you have a one-hundred-percent success rate."

He did. Not that he was one to brag, but no one got away from him. As far as *opening* the business, he'd technically taken over from a friend who'd retired down to the sandy beaches of Florida.

"You're a hunter. You can hunt *him.* You can help me find out who is so determined to hurt me." Intensity vibrated in every word True spoke.

"You aren't going to be hurt." Gruff.

Hope lit her eyes. "You'll help me with my case then? You'll really take the job?"

He wasn't even sure what the job was. What he *was* sure of...True Blakely was staring at him like he was some kind of freaking hero. Growing up, no one had looked at him that way. Despite everything that had happened in the years since he'd left high school, Jake still didn't think he was a hero. He was a bastard who knew how to fight dirty and rough.

But...

What the hell? Why not try something new?

It was the holiday season, after all. And he could do this *one* nice act. Not like it would kill him. And, despite the two perps he'd hunted and tossed back to the cops that day, business was always a little slow before Christmas. Even criminals tried to get off the naughty list occasionally. "I'll look into things for you."

She threw her body against his. "Thank you!" Her breasts crushed to his chest. Her scent wrapped around him. The lush awesomeness that was True pressed against him as she gripped him tightly. "Thank you, thank you! I will pay any price!" True spoke quickly. "I will do anything you want."

Oh, sweets. Do not make promises that I will get you to keep.

"I've been so scared. No one would believe me." She drew back and beamed up at him. "But you do. You believe me."

He wasn't sure what he believed. "I'll investigate and see what I turn up." Maybe the incidents *were* just accidents. Maybe she was overly nervous. He'd figure out the truth. And he'd also get some up close and personal time with True along the way.

Yeah, that would be why I'm always on the naughty list.

She thought she was looking at a hero.

And there he was, imagining how to get her in his bed at the earliest opportunity.

I am such a bastard.

"I..." Her gaze dropped to his mouth. Red immediately stained her cheeks. She seemed to realize that she was gripping his shoulders, and she let him go as she whipped back. "I am grateful."

He didn't move.

"I'll pay whatever your normal hourly rate is."

He didn't have a normal hourly rate. "We'll figure things out." He glanced at his watch. "It's getting close to 8 p.m. Why don't we plan to start investigating first thing tomorrow?" Tomorrow would be Saturday morning.

"You...you said *we*."

He had. Very clearly. Very deliberately.

"You want me to help?"

"Well, it's always easier if you have a witness at the ready. You can walk me through the scene at the museum. You can take me in your house and show me around. So, yep, it's a *we* situation." Working together would also give him more time to spend with the delectable True.

Once more, she beamed at him.

Sonofa—that smile of hers was downright dangerous. It made a man want to do all kinds of things. Like...pretend to be a hero.

"You are fantastic," she praised. "I'm so glad I got up the courage to come and see you!"

She'd needed courage to see him?

"Should I plan to be back here tomorrow morning in order to meet with you?" Eagerness spilled from her. "I can be here anytime you want. I'll...um, I'll just be staying at the motel down the street, so I can—"

He held up his hand. "Say again?"

She licked her lips. "I'll be staying at the motel down the street." She rattled off the name.

A name he was familiar with because the motel was such a notorious piece of crap. The joint should have been condemned long ago.

"I haven't checked in yet, but it's my next stop. I don't feel safe at my house." Hushed. "*Someone has been inside.* I'm sure of it. And I just can't stay there again tonight." She straightened her shoulders. Smiled again. Only this smile seemed forced. "I'll sleep there tonight and be back to meet you at...say seven in the morning?"

"No." He crossed his arms over his chest.

"Oh. Will eight work?"

"No."

She blinked. "What time will work?"

"You're not staying at that no-tell motel, True."

Her cheeks went rosy again. "But it's super close to your office."

"Fuck that." And then he said something he had *not* intended but had definitely fantasized about... "You're coming home with me."

Her eyes went wide. Her lips parted.

"You're staying with *me*." Hell, yes, she was. "You're getting the full-service protection plan." Total bullshit. He had no full-service plan. In fact, he had *no* protection plan. Jake simply hunted the scum of the earth and tossed them back into cells. Case closed. But he could make up things as he went along. Why not? "You can crash at my place, and I can keep an eye on you until we figure out what's happening in your life."

Her long lashes fluttered. "That's so kind of you."

He grunted. *Kind* was not a word normally associated with him. *Heartless. Brutal. Savage.* Sure, those fit.

But this was different. She was different.

And he was going to take True home with him. "Don't

worry," he assured her as he snagged his jacket. Huh. Wait. *She* didn't have a coat. He slid his battered leather jacket over her shoulders. It absolutely swallowed her.

Her hands flew up to hold it in place. Their fingers brushed. Jake pretended he didn't feel the surge of white-hot electricity that zipped through him. That intensity had always been there when they touched, and he'd long since gotten used to acting as if he didn't feel anything.

When I feel everything with True.

"Don't worry," he said again, voice rumbling. "I'll be a perfect gentleman."

"Oh." A nod. She turned away and headed for the door. "That's disappointing."

What? "True?" Her name came out as a ragged growl.

But she'd already opened the door and headed into the small lobby. "I think your Christmas tree is dying. We should water it before we leave."

Screw the tree. He wanted to know...

If True doesn't want me to be a gentleman, then what does she want?

Chapter Two

"When bells ring at Christmas, I make wishes. Is it silly? Yes. Do I still do it? Yes. Will anyone ever stop me? No." – True Blakely

THIS WASN'T HAPPENING.

Okay, well, clearly it *was* happening. She was going home with the one and only Jake Hale. Sexy. Dangerous. Trouble...Jake Hale.

Get a grip, woman. Do not freak out.

She'd already made one serious mistake with him. Letting out that bit about being disappointed in him for behaving like a *gentleman.* Total slipup. But when she was nervous, she often said the wrong thing. And she was super, super nervous.

And afraid.

Not of Jake. Never him. The guy was a hero, after all. All the people in town said so. As soon as she'd gotten back to Rosewood, everyone had been raving about Jake and his outstanding military service. She'd greedily absorbed every tale because...*maybe* she'd once had a thing for him.

What girl *hadn't* been half in love with Jake back in the day? That bad boy appeal had wrecked plenty of hearts. Hers included.

But he wasn't a bad boy. He was a man now. A man who *hunted* bad guys. And he was helping her and—

"Home sweet home," Jake murmured as he opened the door to his condo. He flipped on the lights and waved for her to cross the threshold.

I am spending the night with Jake.

She hurried inside because she was truly curious to see what Jake's home would be like. Honestly, she was curious about everything when it came to him.

True made her way to the middle of his den, then she slowly did a three-hundred-and-sixty-degree turn. The place was immaculate. Really. Super clean. Very high-end. Very masculine.

And just a little cold.

Not the temperature. That was more than fine. But there were no personal touches in his condo. No *soft* touches. Zero decorations, even though they were only days from Christmas. Not even one twinkling light.

"You looking for something?" A polite inquiry from Jake.

Ah... "Who picked out the tree at your office?"

"Perry." A long-suffering sigh. "I swear, I think he pulled the thing out of the trash. Said the tree had plenty of life left in it."

Well, it had *some* life. Not necessarily *plenty*. And she'd watered it before they left so...

"Told him we didn't need that nonsense." Jake pressed a button on a nearby remote, and his gas fireplace immediately flared to life. "But the kid is young, and he was so excited. Then he started playing his damn music." A disgusted shake of his head. "If I'd had to listen to *Jingle Bells* one more time, I think I would have lost my mind."

"You don't like Christmas music or, um, Christmas?"

He turned toward her with a half-grin. "Just call me Ebenezer, but I stopped believing in the magic of Christmas a lifetime ago."

That made her chest feel funny. She tugged his jacket closer even though she should probably be taking it off, and True inched toward him. "Why?"

"Why?" He blinked his intense, I-can-see-straight-into-your-soul eyes. "You really don't know a lot about my life, do you?"

No, she didn't. Just the gossip she'd greedily absorbed. "You were always a private person." Back in school, no one had known his secrets. "But now people know that you were in the military—"

"Sweets, I was in special ops. No one in this town knows what I actually did while I served because those missions are classified and probably always will be." His powerful arms folded over his chest. His head cocked, and the light hit his dark brown hair. His eyes—so dark and deep—held her stare. "Growing up, my life was no picket-fence dream." Flat. Cold. "My dad cut out on us when I was five. My mom had to work two jobs in order to provide for me and my brother. There was barely any money when the holidays came around. If we were lucky, we'd score a tree that looked far too much like that piece of crap Perry hauled into the office. Hell, maybe that's why I don't like the thing. Reminds me too much of my past."

She wasn't inching toward him any longer. Instead, she nearly ran for him. True stopped right in front of Jake.

"My clothes were filled with holes and they were faded as hell not because I was trying to be cool and rebellious, but because we were dirt poor. We had nothing. Holidays were a painful reminder of that fact. So, no, I'm not particularly fond of Christmas and its so-called magic. It's just another holiday to make people who are struggling feel like shit."

Her lower lip trembled.

"What. Are. You. Doing?" Jake seemed utterly horrified as his hands dropped to his sides. "And why the hell did I just tell you all of that?"

What was she doing? Nearly crying. And she was also throwing her arms around him and holding on tight.

"True." He didn't hug her back.

She just hugged him harder.

His hands rose to pat her awkwardly. "True, my family is okay now. Tommy is a lawyer. I've got my own business. We take care of our mom. Right now, she's gone on a cruise we bought for her and her new husband. She is *good*." Another awkward pat. Just his right hand patted her this time. "I shouldn't have told you any of that. I go from telling you nothing to telling you everything. That is not normal."

She pulled back and peered up at him. "I'm sorry Christmas was so difficult for you."

"Forget it. It's in the past. Dead and buried." He hurriedly stepped back. Like three steps. "Even if the Ghost of Christmas Past had to turn up in my office tonight."

True frowned at him.

"Forget it," Jake said again as he turned away. "Long day. You want a beer? Wine? Some food? I'm starving, and I can whip us up some steaks."

"You don't have to cook for me." She trailed after him as Jake made his way into the kitchen. Her gaze took in every detail. White cabinets. White granite countertops. Gourmet kitchen. Like something straight out of a magazine.

"Well, I'm cooking for myself. Doing it for two won't be hard."

A sudden, horrific thought struck her. "Is your girlfriend going to have a problem with me staying with you?" *Of course,* Jake would have a girlfriend. She should go to the motel. One hundred percent.

"Nope." Fast. Very fast. "No girlfriend, so no problem." He held a bottle of wine in his hands. "You got a boyfriend who will have a problem with you staying here?"

"No boyfriend." Just an ex-husband she'd like to forget, thank you very much.

A half-smile teased Jake's lips as he pulled out two glasses and filled them with red wine. He offered one glass to her. "Then I guess it's just us."

Her fingers took the glass. "Just us." The glass trembled in her hand, and some of the wine slid over the edge.

He steadied her hand. "You're safe with me."

She stared into his eyes. Such a deep, compelling gaze.

Such a handsome, dangerous man.

Strong cheekbones. Sharp nose. High forehead. Lips that were sinful. A jaw made of granite. A six-foot-three powerhouse of strength. He'd been impressive as a kid, but with a few laugh lines on his face and with muscles packing his body, Jake Hale was absolutely drop-dead gorgeous now.

"You hired me to protect you, True." He kept holding her hand. Warmth spiraled through her body. "That's exactly what I'll do. You never need to be afraid of me."

"I hired you to find out who is after me." She hadn't hired him to protect her. He was just...doing that.

"Same thing."

Was it?

He let go of her hand. He lifted his glass. "To keeping you safe and stopping the bastard out there."

"I can drink to that." She tapped his glass with her own.

Then she gulped down the wine as fast as she could.

* * *

"WHO WOULD WANT TO HURT YOU?"

Hours had passed. Hours when True had actually felt safe and...dare she say it? Happy. Because being with Jake was actually surprisingly easy. He'd prepared what had to be the best steaks in the world. He'd chatted. He'd joked. He'd been...*charming*. And her guard had lowered. She'd found herself smiling and the tension that had ridden her for days had slowly vanished.

So now she was curled up on his couch, minus her boots and his jacket, with her feet tucked beneath her, and a half-empty wine glass gripped in her hand. She'd been staring into the tempting darkness of his eyes and maybe wondering a bit too much about what his mouth might feel like against hers when the dark rumble of his question had emerged.

Who would want to hurt you? She'd asked herself the same thing so many times lately. And the answer was always the same. "I-I don't know."

"No enemies? No exes who just didn't want to let go?" He didn't hold a wine glass. One arm was stretched along the back of the couch. The other rested near his side. His watchful gaze never left her face.

She put down her glass. "I'm divorced, but my ex is hardly the kind of man who would try to kill me."

"You sure about that? Sometimes, you think you know

someone..." His words trailed away. She could have sworn his gaze heated. Then he finished, "And you discover you never really knew the person at all."

"Richard is a prosecutor in Atlanta. He puts criminals away. He *isn't* one." Though there were plenty of sins that he did choose to commit, *killing* wasn't one of them.

"You sure about that?"

"We divorced. He didn't—didn't put some kind of hit on me!"

"Why did you divorce?"

She blinked. "Irreconcilable differences."

He just waited.

"He wanted to fuck his legal secretary, and I had a problem with that. An irreconcilable problem." Her mouth dropped open after the stark confession. Oh, wow. She had *not* meant to share one of the most humiliating moments of her life. *I found them together when I took him dinner because Richard was working a late-night shift on a big case. They were kissing on his desk.* She'd dropped the food. Chinese. It had spilled all across the floor as she'd stared at him and felt every single one of her dreams crash around her. And it had hurt extra hard because...

No, do not go there. Don't think about it right now.

"He was married to you." Jake cocked his head to the right. "And he wanted to fuck someone else?"

Pain burned through her.

"What a fucking idiot." A pause. "Want me to go beat the hell out of him?"

A shocked laugh sputtered out of her. "No!"

"The offer will always be on the table." He leaned toward her. His hand reached out and curled under her chin. "He hurt you. I can hurt him back. You say the word."

True found she couldn't say any word. She could only

look into the darkness of his eyes and then...Her gaze dropped to his mouth.

"You went back to your maiden name," Jake noted.

"I wanted my old life back. My name. My town." So she'd turned away from everything in Atlanta and moved back to Rosewood. Rosewood was home. Safety. Or, it had been. Until the incidents had started.

His thumb brushed along her lower lip.

Her breath stuttered out.

"You've been here a year," Jake noted.

Her eyes widened. "How do you know that?" Oh, no. Had her tongue just *accidentally* brushed along the tip of his thumb? It had. And why was she letting him touch her this way? She should get up. Move away. Put some space between them. She would have, too. If his touch hadn't felt so good.

"People talk. The town princess coming home was a big deal."

"I'm hardly the town princess."

His gaze fell to her mouth.

Is Jake Hale about to kiss me?

Her heart slammed into her chest.

"What about the men you've been with since your divorce?"

"What men?"

He frowned at her.

Oh, crap. Hello, more embarrassment. "I, um, my social life hasn't been very active. Been busy with the move." *Lie.* She'd unpacked immediately after her move. "I've been busy with the new job." Another lie. The job at the museum kept her busy, yes, but there would have been time to date. And... "I suck at dating." A dismal truth. "I'm just not very good at it. Trust is hard for me, and I don't...I haven't." He watched her with a faint furrow between his eyes, as if he still didn't understand, so she rushed out, "I haven't been with anyone since my divorce, so there is definitely no jealous ex out there who is thinking if he can't have me, then no one can."

Silence.

"I mean," she cleared her throat and ignored the burn she could feel in her cheeks, "if that was your suspicion, it's wrong." She pulled away from him and rose. That had been way too awkward.

"You haven't fucked anyone in a year?" Disbelief filled the rumble that was his voice.

True winced. "I haven't *dated* anyone since my divorce became final. The divorce itself took about six months. So, technically, I haven't, um, had sex with anyone in a year and a half."

"Sonofabitch."

Yes, indeed. It had rather been a sonofabitch. "I should get to bed. It's late." And she'd revealed enough painful personal information for one night. True glanced around. "If you could just point me in the direction of your guest room...?"

"Don't have one."

Her stare flew back to him.

He shrugged. "It's a one-bedroom condo. Got a king bed in my room."

An image of him in that king bed immediately flooded through her mind. And in that image, she was with him. Tangled in black sheets with him. Breaking that year and a half streak.

Once more, True cleared her throat. "The couch will be great. I can sleep here tonight."

Lazily, he rose. And stood beside her. When Jake was

right next to her, True was vividly conscious of just how big he was. It wasn't just that he was tall. It was that he was muscled. Powerful. And he seemed to absolutely surround her.

"Sweets," he murmured. "If I let a lady sleep on the couch while my happy ass stretched out in a king-size bed, then I damn well wouldn't be a gentleman, would I?"

Her head tipped back as she stared up at him.

"And I think I told you before that I would play the gentleman."

And I think that I told you before...That's disappointing. But she would not say those words to him. Mostly because she could not. True wasn't the bold one. Wasn't particularly brave. And making the first move with a man like Jake? A guy who oozed sex appeal and testosterone?

He was way out of her league. She would not know how to handle him.

But I'd certainly like to try.

True bit her lower lip. "I can really take the couch. It will fit me better. You're too big for it."

"I'll be fine. You're sleeping in the bed." An order.

"You've already done so much for me! You took my case, you gave me a safe place to stay, and you made dinner for me!" A desperate shake of her head. "I can't take your bed, too."

His eyes gleamed at her. "It's a done deal, True. Go to bed. We'll start our investigation in the morning."

"Arguing with you isn't going to work?"

"Nope."

She took a step back. "Then...thank you. For taking my case. For the place to stay. For dinner. And for your bed."

His head inclined.

True retreated one more step. "Are you always this kind?"

"Absolutely not. Typically, I'm a straight-up bastard." He pointed to the right. "First room is the bathroom. Second room is the bedroom."

She edged toward the right. "If you're usually a bastard, why are you being so nice to me?" True turned away from him.

"Because it's you."

His low words stopped her.

"Want to hear a secret, sweets?"

She looked back over her shoulder. "Why do you call me that?"

"Because you've always smelled so sweet."

Her shampoo. He must be talking about her strawberry-scented shampoo. She'd used the stuff forever.

"And I bet you'd taste even sweeter."

Her eyes widened.

"That secret I just mentioned? Well, what you might not have known was that I had quite the crush on you in high school."

He had *not* just said that to her. Not about how she might taste and certainly not about having a crush on her. Casually, she reached down and gave her thigh a little pinch.

Not dreaming. This is real.

"You'll need something to sleep in."

Actually, yes, she did. The only clothing she had with her—it was the dress she currently wore. She'd spontaneously made the decision to stay at the motel after arriving at his office. The fear had been too much, and True just hadn't been able to stand the thought of going back to her house. *I know someone is watching me.* So she had no extra clothes. Zero toiletries.

"Feel free to borrow one of my t-shirts. Top drawer of the dresser." Then he reached down and pulled off the shirt he was wearing.

Muscles. Abs. A ten-pack, at least.

His hand went to the buckle of his jeans. "Just gonna get comfortable," he murmured.

He was aroused. Very aroused. Because her eyes had dropped to the front of his jeans automatically—when his hands moved, her eyes had moved, too. There was no missing the long, thick cock that pushed forward.

"If you need me, True, I'll be right out here."

He undid the buckle. She bolted for the bedroom. True shut the door—more like slammed it—even as her heart raced in her chest. Jake Hale had just said that he'd had a crush on her. Jake Hale wondered what it would be like to kiss her.

Jake Hale had an insane body.

And I want to know what it's like to kiss him, too.

Only, instead of giving in to the need that had been inside True since her teenage years, she'd just run from him.

Story of her life. Always being too afraid to reach out for what she really wanted. Even when he was right there.

WELL, he'd certainly fucked that up.

Jake sprawled on the couch—with his legs dangling off the left armrest and over the edge because the freaking thing *was* too small for him—and he glared at the ceiling. He had True in his home. She'd been smiling and chatting with him.

Then he'd fucked things to hell and back. Just confessing about the old crush had sent her running at double-time speed away from him. Fine. Message received. Despite the cues that he'd *thought* he might be picking up on, True was not interested in him.

One hundred percent, not.

He lifted his wrist and glared at the glow-in-the-dark watch screen. Midnight. It was gonna be one long night. He hauled off the watch and dropped it on the floor beside him. His dick was hard and aching, and no relief would be in sight.

Way to send her running. He should have kept his stupid mouth shut.

Creak.

Jake tensed. Had that just been the bedroom door opening?

The floor squeaked. He knew that squeaky spot. It was three steps in front of his bedroom.

He did not move. Maybe True was just heading to the kitchen for a glass of water or something. Just because he heard her tiptoeing around, it did not mean that the woman was coming to talk to him. *Definitely* did not mean that she'd suddenly decided she couldn't live without him for another moment and that she planned to jump him.

"Jake?" A hushed whisper. The living room was dark, but he could make out her shadowy form as she stood near the side of the sofa. "Are you asleep?"

Hell, no. He was awake and in frustrated, sexual agony.

"Bad idea," she murmured. True began to turn away.

His hand flew out and locked around her wrist. "I like bad ideas." Loved them, in fact. His favorite ideas were bad. "You got something you need to say?"

"I..." A soft sigh. "I have a confession."

Go on. He squinted as he tried to see her better in the dark. Was she wearing his t-shirt? Oh, yes, he thought that she was. *Sexy as hell.*

"You weren't the only one with a crush in high school." A husky reveal. "I watched you, far more than I should have. And I might've had some fantasies about you."

Fantasies? His dick saluted extra hard.

"I had a crush on you. And I have often wondered...just how you would taste, too."

How was a man supposed to resist a confession like that one?

"Just wanted you to know," she added, a little breathless. True tried to tug her wrist from his grip. "Uh, good night."

Uh, *no.*

In a flash, Jake shot to his feet. He'd ditched his belt and shoes after shedding his shirt, but he still had on his jeans. He didn't let go of her wrist. Instead, Jake hauled her closer. "Let's settle this mystery," he said against her mouth.

Then he kissed her.

And lost his mind.

Chapter Three

"Who needs mistletoe? I'm kissing her. Right here. Right now." – Jake Hale

Jake was kissing her. She was kissing him. And it was the most incredible kiss of her life. Off the charts hot. Body scorching. Lust ignited within True. He'd freed her wrist, and both of her hands flew up to tightly grab his powerful shoulders as she tried to pull him closer to her.

A kiss wasn't supposed to feel like this, was it? Because if it was...oh, if it was, then she'd been doing it all wrong for years. Because a kiss had never, ever been this explosive. This body-melting. This—this *panty-wetting*.

She was turned on. Hot and wet for him.

From a kiss.

True jerked her head back. She stared at his shadowy form in shock even as her panting breaths filled the air.

"Was it good for you, too?" he growled.

"That was the best kiss of my life," she told him honestly, breathless. "Can we do it again?"

He growled once more. Or cursed. Maybe both? Then his mouth was taking hers again with a feverish intensity. As if he wanted to gobble her right up. He stroked and teased with his tongue, and she moaned helplessly even as her body rubbed eagerly against his.

His hands curled around her waist. He lifted her up—like she weighed nothing and that was even *hotter* because he was so strong—and she gasped against his mouth. He stole her breath. Gave her his.

So sexy.

"Wrap your legs around my waist," he ordered.

Oh, yes, sure. She could do that. She *did* do that. And then he started carrying her back through the condo. Back toward—the bedroom? Yes, they were heading toward the bedroom. Things had accelerated from zero to explosion super, super fast. This was way beyond the norm for her.

Was it the norm for him? Was this like a typical Friday night? You kiss a woman, and she goes crazy for you?

Uncertainty blossomed in her even as he lowered her onto the bed. A king-size bed that did, indeed, have black sheets. She'd left the bedside lamp glowing when she finally got the nerve to exit the room and tiptoe into the den for her big confession. Now, she could see Jake and seeing him was...

He looks like a predator. Like he really does want to eat me alive.

He stood beside the bed. His hands were at his sides. His eyes on her. Or, rather, on her legs. The oversized t-shirt she'd taken from his drawer had risen up, and it skimmed the tops of her thighs. His focus was one hundred percent clear.

Did we just go from a kiss to sex? "We haven't even gone out on a date," she blurted.

His gaze rose to her face. Lust burned in his stare. "You want me to date you?"

That was the normal order of things, wasn't it? At least in her world. Her world of limited experience. Was this the part where she should confess to having limited partners? As in, two total? One in college, and then after—the guy she'd gone on to foolishly marry?

"Date you before I fuck you?" A harsh growl from Jake.

She jerked upright into a sitting position and immediately yanked the hem of the shirt down. "It was a kiss!"

He watched her with those blazing, dark eyes of his.

"I don't...even if it was the best kiss ever, I'm not ready for—" True stopped. She tried to regain control of herself and the situation. "I don't know what's happening."

"I didn't bring you in here to fuck you."

He...hadn't?

"I brought you in here so I wouldn't fuck you."

Um, he'd brought her to the bedroom, put her on the bed...so they *wouldn't* have sex? She was completely confused. And...True notched up her chin. "I don't remember asking you to fuck me."

He took a step away from the bed. "My control with you is razor thin. You tasted like my fantasies, and now I just want to taste *all* of you. Every single inch." His gaze had dropped. Once more. Focused on the juncture of her thighs. "Over and over again. Until you come against my mouth."

Oh. Wow. "Uh, Jake?"

"You're not ready for that. You're not ready for me."

She could agree with one hundred percent certainty

that she was not, in fact, ready for him. But she still wanted him. Very badly. Their kiss—kisses—had unlocked something within her. Something that maybe she'd been chaining up for far too long. Playing by the rules her whole life had gotten her heartache. What would it be like to forget those rules? Just once?

"You're scared. You're running on adrenaline. And I will not be the bastard who takes advantage of you. That's not who I am." Another step back. "I am going to leave you, safe and sound, in *my* bed. You get some rest tonight. Something tells me that you have not experienced a good night's sleep in a while. Tomorrow, you'll wake up with a clear head. And if you still want me tomorrow, then I will fucking date you. I'll play by your rules." His eyes glittered. "Then I *will* have you."

Her heart still raced far too fast.

He turned and headed for the door.

"Jake?"

He stilled.

"I'm going to want you tomorrow. I've wanted you since I was sixteen, and that want hasn't changed. So I don't particularly think I'll wake up in the morning and the need will suddenly be gone."

Jake glanced over his shoulder at her.

She licked her lips. "So I guess I'll be having *you* soon."

His jaw clenched. "Ice skating," he bit out.

"Excuse me?" Was that some sort of euphemism that she was not getting?

"We'll go ice skating for our first date."

Not any euphemism. He meant actual ice skating. And an actual date. A gentle glow seemed to build inside of her. "Sounds like a plan."

His head jerked. Then he faced forward. He crossed over the threshold—

"Good night, Jake."

His body paused. "Good night, sweets."

* * *

Jake hauled the door shut. Then he looked down at his hand. His fingers were shaking. Need flooded through every cell of his body. He could never, ever remember wanting someone this much.

She's not just someone.

True Blakely.

And he'd kissed her, and she'd told him it was the best kiss of her life.

"Cold shower," Jake muttered. *"Cold. Shower."*

Yep, just as he'd thought before...it was going to be one long-ass night.

* * *

If Rosewood had a fancy part of town, then, of course, True would live in it. The two-story house waited on a small cul-de-sac. Gated yards. Perfect lawns. Houses that gleamed and shined in the morning light.

Houses that were far, far away from the home he'd grown up in.

They'd been worlds apart as teens.

Now their worlds were colliding.

True doesn't know it, but I'm not some piss-poor punk any longer. He'd more than made his own fortune over the years. He could afford to buy the biggest house in town, if he wanted. He could have a luxury car. Five of them. Go on trips to the best places in the world.

But he didn't do that shit. Because he was fine just as he was.

Alone?

The last thought slithered through his mind. Might have made him shift uncomfortably.

"I'll just...change clothes real fast." True was back in her red dress as she bent over the front door's lock. "Give me a few moments to freshen up, and we can hit the museum. I'll show you exactly where I was when the crash occurred."

He trailed behind her as she opened the door and slipped inside. Anticipation filled him because he was quite curious about what the inside of True's house would look like and—

And it looked as if Christmas had exploded.

He nodded. Yep. That fit.

She'd wrapped green garland—with red bows—around the banisters that led up to the second floor. Two small, fully decorated trees were strategically placed on either side of the staircase. He could have sworn that he even smelled cinnamon hanging in the air. Of course, the woman's house would smell delicious. How could it not?

"I'll run upstairs. Please, make yourself at home."

He strolled toward what he took to be her den. His eyes went first to the massive Christmas tree near her fireplace. Eight feet tall? Ten? And how had she gotten the bows to flow down the tree that way? His gaze followed the ribbon and bows as they twisted and flowed down to the bottom of—

Shock rolled through him. "True?"

He could hear her steps on the stairs.

"True!" Louder. "I need you."

And those steps immediately rushed back down the staircase. Her boots padded over the hardwood of the small foyer and then into the den as she breathlessly asked, "What is it?"

"Oh, you know, the usual. A giant Christmas tree. A stocking hung with care." He took a step back so she could take in the full sights in the den. "And a dead body tucked in with the holiday presents." When he made that last, bald statement, Jake was watching her face.

Absolute horror flashed across her expression even as she opened her mouth and screamed.

Jake nodded. "Right, guessing he is *not* supposed to be there."

"What?" Another shriek. "Of course, he is *not supposed to be there!"*

"Then we have a problem." When she lunged toward what was clearly a dead body, complete with a bullet hole in his chest—did the woman think she was gonna help the guy, now?—Jake wrapped his arms around her stomach and hauled her back. "Let's not touch the body, sweets. Better to not contaminate the scene."

"There is a dead body under my Christmas tree!" True shrieked.

Jake lifted her up and carried her back toward the front door.

"Jake, there is a dead body under my Christmas tree!" Slightly hysterical.

"Yep, I did notice it." Hard to miss it, in fact. "Pro tip, sweets, I'd probably throw out all of the presents that have blood on them."

She shuddered in his arms.

Chapter Four

"I'm dreaming of...a Christmas that doesn't include a dead body. Is that really so much to ask? And why the heck was he under my Christmas tree?"
– True Blakely

THE POLICE STATION WAS FESTIVE. TRUE WAS TRYING—extremely hard—to look on the bright side of things. Sure, it was difficult, considering that she was in a police interrogation room and the detective at the table kept casting her suspicious glances.

As if, you know, she'd committed murder.

"I didn't," she mumbled to no one in particular as her hands clutched the cold cup of coffee in front of her.

At least the police station is festive. Red and gold garland had been hung up everywhere. Christmas music played in the lobby. And...

She was in interrogation. Because there was a dead body under her tree. True's shoulders slumped.

"You have no idea who the victim might be?"

She blinked at the detective. Detective Harris Avery. She'd talked to him before, when she'd been trying to convince the police that someone was trying to kill her. Harris had actually gone to school with her. She, Harris, and Jake had all been in the same graduating class.

She'd thought their shared past might make Harris more likely to hear her out when she'd tried to explain what had been happening.

It hadn't. He'd told her that the cops were stretched too thin. That they didn't have enough personnel to come and check out her house. That accidents happened. Harris had told her to be more careful. In other words, he'd provided zero help.

But Jake helped me. Jake, who was sitting silently beside her in interrogation. He was helping. He'd believed her when no one else had.

And, now, she had a dead body in her den. Suddenly, the cops seemed to be taking her very seriously. Murder made things serious. But as to who the dead man was... "No clue."

"You'd never seen him before?" Harris pushed.

The dead man's image flashed through her mind. Dirty blond hair. Slightly twisted nose, as if it had been broken before. Rounded chin. Young—maybe early twenties? He'd been wearing all black. Black sweatshirt. Black pants. Even black sneakers.

She had stared at the dead body in horror and with zero recognition. "I'd never seen him before, not until I saw his body under my tree."

Harris narrowed his green eyes. "Where were you last night," he asked, never taking his gaze from her, "between the hours of eleven p.m. and one a.m.?"

"I—"

"Is that what the ME is giving you as the time of death?" Jake wanted to know.

Harris shifted his attention to Jake. "Okay, I'm still confused. Why the hell are you here? Not like you're the woman's lawyer. And I'm pretty sure she hasn't jumped bail so what gives?"

"Oh, God." A gasp from True as she released the coffee cup. "Do I *need* a lawyer?"

"No," Jake was adamant. "You don't. Because you have an airtight alibi." A pause. "Me."

She hadn't thought that Harris's eyes could narrow more. They did.

"You?" Harris questioned.

"Yep. Me. I was with True last night." Jake rolled one shoulder. Like the admission was nothing. Like he provided alibis for *murder suspects* all the time.

Harris's gaze dipped back and forth between them. "You two went out? Maybe you were at a restaurant? A party? On some kind of date last night?"

True shook her head.

Jake let out a sigh as he leaned forward. "She was at my place. In my bed."

Harris's jaw dropped.

"She was with me," Jake continued, "from about eight p.m. last night until this morning when I *went with True* to her house. She wanted to change clothes."

Oh, jeez. That made it sound like—like they had—

"I am the one who discovered the body," Jake stated, voice calm and cool and so very controlled. "And, no, I didn't touch anything near the dead guy."

"You didn't try to help him?" Harris asked.

Jake laughed. "Uh, *no.* You can't help the dead. *Clearly,* he was dead. Had been that way for hours. I backed away. Got True out of there. And, like the responsible citizens we are, we called the cops." His hands flattened on the table. "We've cooperated. We've helped with your investigation. But this grilling BS with True has to stop. She's obviously the victim."

"Uh, some would say the vic was the dead man in her house—" Harris began.

"How'd he get in?" Jake demanded. "The front entrance showed no signs of tampering. I'm betting the same can't be the case for her back door. Or maybe a window. And I *saw* the ski mask on the floor near the dead guy."

Wow. What ski mask? She hadn't noticed it. But Jake had hauled her—carried her—out of the house fast after she'd seen the body.

"You know that someone has been terrorizing True." Anger rumbled beneath Jake's words. "Only instead of helping her, you left her on her own." That wasn't just anger vibrating in his voice. It was quiet rage. "If I hadn't been with her last night, if True had been home, just what in the hell do you think that bastard would have done? You think a bastard breaks in, wearing a ski mask, because he's there to fucking sing Christmas carols to her?"

True realized she was holding her breath.

I hadn't intended to be home last night. I was going to stay at a motel. I was so sure I could feel someone watching me.

Jake's head turned toward her. "You told me that you felt like someone had been in your house before."

She nodded.

"And you told the same story to the cops before you came to me."

"I...told Harris."

Jake's head swung back toward Harris. "And you didn't investigate? What the fuck?"

"Do you *know* how many cases I'm working?" Harris jerked a hand through his reddish-brown hair.

"I don't give a shit about your other cases. I'm here for her. True is what matters to me." A tight, angry pause. "You should have helped her when she first came to the station."

Harris grimaced.

But Jake wasn't done. "The asshole dead beneath her tree? The one near the discarded *ski mask?*" Jake gritted out.

True flinched.

"He could have been in her home over and over. He could have been sneaking in to watch her while she slept."

Her stomach knotted. *Hello, new nightmares.*

"He was stalking her," Jake continued relentlessly. "Terrorizing her. If she had been home last night, *she* could be the dead one beneath the—"

"Don't," True whispered even as her hand flew out and curled around his arm.

Jake tensed beneath her touch.

"I'm okay," she added.

He released a low breath. His head turned once more toward her. "It fucking pisses me off, sweets," he rumbled. "You should never have been threatened. Cops aren't doing shit. Interrogating you? Acting like you're the perp when you've been the vic all along? Screw that. From here on out, count on *me*."

"Well, damn." A surprised exclamation from Harris. "It really is like that with you two?"

"Screw yourself, Harris," Jake ordered without looking away from True.

Her eyes widened. She didn't think he was supposed to tell a detective to go screw himself.

A knock sounded at the door.

"I'll get that. You two just keep doing whatever it is that the two of you do." Harris shoved back his chair. He marched for the door. Hauled it open. "Don't leave the room, though. We aren't finished." The door softly clicked closed behind him.

Her breath expelled in long, ragged sigh. "I've never been in an interrogation before."

"That's because you're one of those good girls who has never done jack shit wrong before. And understand this, you haven't done anything wrong *now*. You are the victim." Jake turned his body fully toward her. Then he leaned forward and pulled her against him in a tight hug.

She had to blink quickly because, oh, she'd needed a hug. Really, really badly. That had been her first dead body. And it had...smelled. And looked stiff. *And blood had been on the presents.* Blood from the bullet wound on the dead man.

"Since you have never been in an interrogation room, there is something you need to know," Jake rasped against her ear. His breath blew lightly against the shell of her ear and made her tremble. Not in a bad way. "That mirror to the left? It's a one-way mirror. That means someone can be in there watching, so be very careful what you say." He pulled back.

True realized that the hug had been fake. Just a cover so he could warn her about the mirror. But she didn't need a warning. True wrapped her arms around her body. She was still wearing the same dress, dammit. Who did a woman have to kill for new clothes?

Not funny, True. Not. Funny.

"I haven't done anything wrong," she said, loudly and clearly, in case someone was watching from the other side of that mirror. "I don't have anything to hide. I don't know who that man was. I don't know how he got inside my house. I don't know why—why he would want to hurt me."

"Some people are just sick sonsofbitches." Jake's hand rose and pressed to her cheek. "You are safe, and you're staying that way."

"Who was he?" His touch warmed skin that she hadn't even realized was cold. "And who killed him?"

Determination hardened his expression. "We're going to find out, I swear it." His gaze fell to her mouth. "You could have been there." Low. "You could have been alone." He dropped his hand. "*You could have been hurt.*"

Now she was the one to touch his cheek. "I wasn't."

His head turned. His lips skimmed over her palm.

True sucked in a breath.

The door swung open. "Ah, Jake?" Harris cleared his throat. "If you're not too busy in there, how about a word? A word *out here,* with me?"

Jake stared at True. How could dark eyes burn so much? "You will not be hurt," he vowed.

She nodded. Not getting hurt sounded like a great plan to her. Top-notch. Fabulous.

He rose and headed for the door.

She grabbed for her cold coffee again.

You will not be hurt.

No, she wouldn't be. Jake was on her side. Yes, a dead man was under her tree. *Don't think about him. Stop seeing his image in your mind.* But she wasn't alone in this nightmare.

She had the best bounty hunter in town at her side.

She had the bad boy from her past...and, now, he was going to protect her.

* * *

"WHAT IN THE hell is going on?" Harris questioned as soon as the interrogation room door closed. He pointed to the closed door as they stood in the hallway. "You and True? *You and True*? Since when?"

Jake crossed his arms over his chest and put his back to the door. "Why the hell didn't you tell me she was in trouble?" A quick glance assured Jake that they appeared to be the only ones in the corridor.

Harris blinked. "What? Why would I tell you?"

"Because I would have liked to have fucking known."

Harris retreated a step. "How the hell would *I* know that? No, no, back up. Stop. First, I don't disclose personal information about victims who come to the station—"

"So you thought she was a victim, and you did nothing?" The rage broke free again. He'd tried to keep the fire of his fury contained, but every single time he thought about what *could* have happened to True, his blood boiled in his veins.

Harris gripped a manila file with his right hand. "I thought she was having accidents! *Accidents*. As in, random shit that happens to people! Look, when she was supposedly pushed off the sidewalk and into the road, there were no witnesses. No witnesses at the museum, either. I ordered patrols to circle through her neighborhood as a precaution, but there was nothing to indicate she was in actual danger."

"Nothing to indicate it, huh?" Jake raised one brow. "What about the dead body?"

Harris squeezed his eyes shut. "The dead body changes things."

"Yeah, buddy, I thought it might."

Harris cracked open his eyes and sighed.

They were, in fact, buddies. They hadn't been back in their high school days. They'd been rivals then. Harris's pompous ass had annoyed Jake most days. But when they'd met again as adults, things had been different. Harris was a rule follower—too much of one, as far as Jake was concerned. Harris needed to learn that rules should be bent some days. But he was an honest cop. Harris tried to help. Usually, he succeeded.

Not in True's case. "You sent her away." Something Jake would not forgive. "She could have been hurt."

"Yeah. That shit is gonna haunt me." Harris lifted the file. "We got an ID on the dead guy. Dylan Dunn. He was bad news."

Jake swiped the file. He flipped it open and whistled when he saw the rap sheet. A very long rap sheet. "Shoplifting, petty theft, B&Es, assault..." He focused on the picture of the perp. "Dylan was certainly making his way up the crime ladder, wasn't he?"

"He'd been in and out of jail since he was sixteen years old. Last known address was in Atlanta," Harris pointed out.

Atlanta. Where True had just happened to live for several years.

"You think he got obsessed with her there? Their paths must have crossed. Something locked and loaded the guy on her," Harris added as the faint lines near his mouth deepened. "I know True said that she didn't know him, but he clearly knew her."

Jake lowered the file. "You're thinking he was the one

behind the shove in the street and the attack at her museum."

"Isn't that what *you're* thinking?"

Now that he'd seen the rap sheet, yeah. "The last assault charge was from an ex-girlfriend who said Dylan shoved her down a flight of stairs when he got mad. So, yes, I could see this prick shoving True into the path of an oncoming car."

"One of the uniforms found a local motel room registered to him. A search is being conducted there now. I'll let you know what we turn up."

"Appreciate that." Reluctantly, he handed the file back to Harris. "So who killed the bastard?"

"I was wondering the same thing." Harris stared back at him.

It took a moment for the suspicion in Harris's gaze to register, and when it did, laughter burst from Jake.

"And that is not the response I was expecting," Harris groused.

Jake laughed harder. "Oh, man." He calmed down a bit. "You think I'd kill a guy and leave him beneath True's Christmas tree? If I'd killed him—"

The door opened behind him.

"—there would have been no body left to find," Jake finished.

Jake caught True's gasp. Figured she would've heard the last part. Oh, well. He'd just been stating the truth. He could kill a man and leave no trace behind. Harris would be well aware of that fact, and now, True would understand, too. Jake's stare remained on Harris. In this case, though, he was innocent. "I didn't kill the guy." Just so they were all clear. "Besides, like I told you, I was with True. All night." He was her alibi, and she was his.

Harris shifted his focus over Jake's shoulder. "That correct? You were with him all night?"

Okay, now this was the dicey part. Technically, they hadn't been together, not *all night.* Because his dumb ass had been a gentleman. So he'd been in the den, she'd been in the bedroom, and if she confessed that particular bit of information, then his buddy might just think Jake had been free to slip out and off the punk at her house—

"I was in his bed," True's prim voice responded. "All night long."

Truth. A very carefully worded truth.

She pressed her hand to Jake's shoulder. He obligingly moved to the side so she could fully exit the interrogation room. Only True didn't go far. She just moved closer to him. The sweet smell of strawberries teased his nose.

Yeah, I could freaking gobble her right up. Something on his to-do list. After, apparently, he *dated* the woman.

"Well, this has to be like a Christmas dream coming true for you." Harris pointed the file toward Jake. He also continued, with his very big mouth, "Finally getting the girl of your fantasies, huh? That's a Christmas miracle."

Jake stared at him. Just stared. Harris could be such a pain in his ass.

Beside him, True sucked in a sharp breath.

"Except for the body," Harris hastened to add. "That is not a Christmas miracle. That is a Christmas homicide, and rest assured, I will get to the bottom of this mystery."

Oh, yeah, Jake felt all kinds of reassured.

"I'm to assume that you'll be sticking close to True from here on out?" Harris asked as he stopped pointing with the damn file and dropped his hand back to his side.

"You assume correctly." They had a murderer on the

loose. One who'd been in True's house. Good thing Jake excelled at tracking down killers and criminals.

"The ME is working on her report. I'll be sure to give you the highlights when Sara is done." Harris lowered his voice as he revealed, "Based on rigor mortis, though, we're thinking the vic was shot around midnight. And it doesn't take a degree in medicine to realize the guy was shot in the heart."

"No neighbors heard the shot?" Jake had to ask the question.

Harris shook his head. "Could be they were sound sleepers. And the houses aren't *that* close together on the cul-de-sac."

Or it could be that a professional had fired the shot to kill the SOB. *A professional with a silencer?* Shit, if that was the case, things were getting very, very complicated.

Harris's gaze slid to True. "You *sure* you didn't know the guy?"

She shook her head.

"The name Dylan Dunn means nothing to you?" Harris pushed.

"Is that—is that who he was?"

Harris nodded.

"The guy's last known address was Atlanta," Jake told her.

True gave a start of surprise. "I'm sorry, but I don't know him. There are a whole lot of people in Atlanta." She grimaced. "I have no idea why he was in my house, and I have *no clue* who killed him."

"But we'll be finding out," Jake promised.

"I knew you were going to say that." A sigh from Harris. "You get that I'm the one with the badge, right? Told you a million times, if you want to solve the cases, you should join the force. The job was made for you."

"I like making my own rules." He'd followed enough of them during his special ops time. He wasn't ready to sit behind a desk and take orders from police brass.

"No, you just like being a badass who gets to stalk his prey. That shit is scary." A uniform appeared at the end of the hallway. Harris immediately straightened and raised his voice as he said, "That's all the questions for now. I'll be sure and contact you for follow-up."

Jake saluted him. "Yeah, you do that. We'll be waiting." Then he threaded his fingers with True's and began walking down the hallway and toward the exit. They'd taken five steps when...

Harris snapped his fingers. "Sorry! Forgot to mention—True, your home is a crime scene. I'm gonna suggest you find another place to crash for the next twenty-four—maybe forty-eight—hours while the techs do their work."

Jake turned his head to look at True. She was already looking at him. "She'll be with me." Hadn't they already covered that he had no intention of letting her out of his sight?

Not with a killer on the loose.

Talk about your nightmare-before-Christmas situation.

Ho, ho...homicide.

Chapter Five

"When you deck the halls, you don't typically leave a dead body under the Christmas tree. That's just...not very festive." –True Blakely

"It's also a murder, sweets. A fucking murder." – Jake Hale

"I WAS STANDING RIGHT HERE." THEY WERE IN THE museum's grand exhibit hall. One she'd been tirelessly prepping because the traveling Egyptology display was slated to open after the new year. Thankfully, she'd changed into extra clothes that she had in her work locker. Yoga pants. A sweatshirt. Comfortable tennis shoes and not her boots. "I was the only one in the area. All of the other staff members—except our head of security, Robert Moss—had gone home for the night." She glanced around at the two elaborate sarcophagi that had been carefully arranged in the exhibit hall. One to the left. The other to the right.

They were the centerpieces of the display. "There are over one hundred treasures in the traveling collection." Including a royal mask that was behind security glass on the center wall. "But the piece that nearly fell on me wasn't part of the collection, thank goodness. That would have been an insurance nightmare." She shuddered just imaging the paperwork.

"Yeah, total nightmare." Jake's droll response. "Especially if you'd, I don't know, *died*."

She cut him a quick glance.

"What fell?" Jake asked.

"A large, white column. Not ancient Egyptian. Just decorative, but very heavy." Heavy enough to have caused serious injury if it had hit her. "It's designed with a light inside to set the mood for the display."

"Got to set the mood." He rocked back on his heels. "So you were standing here, prepping the exhibit all by yourself, and the column just fell?"

"It *couldn't* have fallen on its own. That's what I tried to explain to Harris. I built the column. It was sturdy. You'd have to push it—hard—in order to make it fall. Not like I'd have some accident-waiting-to-happen situation in here for museum visitors." She took safety very seriously. The protection of museum visitors was always a priority for her.

"And this particular column was positioned over here, in front of the curtains?" Jake's hand waved toward said curtains.

She nodded.

He moved toward the wall—the wall lined with thick, black curtains. He lifted the curtains and studied the small space behind the billowing fabric. "Easy enough for someone to hide back here."

Yes, someone could hide behind the curtains, and that

fact creeped her out. The idea that someone had been there while she'd been working her late nights made fear slither through her veins.

"He just would have waited for the perfect moment." Jake let the curtains fall back into place as his gaze swept the large exhibit hall. "I see there are two security cameras in this area."

Her lips pressed together. "Yes, but they weren't operational that night. They are brand new—actually, they still aren't up and running. The whole system at the museum is in the process of being upgraded."

"That's unfortunate."

Understatement. Before she'd started work at the museum, there had been a few *very* old cameras in the place. Truth be told, the museum had been dying. So many of the wonderful artifacts had been boxed up in storage. She'd made it her mission to bring the place to life once again. Using the connections she'd made while working at a larger museum in Atlanta, True had been able to score the traveling Egyptian exhibit. She'd been planning to use that exhibit to get people in the doors. Then she'd been hoping the good folks in Rosewood would come back to see all of the wonderful art and artifacts that she'd planned to display once again. *Everything is coming out of storage.*

"And nothing was caught on any other security cams at the facility?" Jake pressed.

She shook her head. The very lack of anything—anyone—being caught on the other, older cameras had been one of the reasons Harris seemed so certain she'd imagined things.

Just an accident.

Just an accident, her ass.

The dead man's image flashed through her mind. Dizziness suddenly had her trembling.

Jake's hand closed around hers. "You okay?"

She sucked in a deep breath. Then one more. "I've never found a dead body before."

"I could say you get used to them." His hand squeezed hers. "But that would be a lie. It's gonna haunt you for a while."

"Was he there to hurt me?" He must have been.

"Well, I'm thinking he wasn't there to deliver Christmas cookies so..." Jake winced. "Bad joke. Yeah, sweets. With his rap sheet, his intentions were damn dangerous. I'm glad you weren't there." He released her hand.

But she grabbed his hand right back. "What did Harris mean?"

He looked at their hands. Then at her face. One brow rose in query.

Right. She should explain herself better. "When he said it was like a Christmas miracle for you." She bit her lower lip.

His gaze fell to her lip.

Heated.

And her heartbeat raced. *Settle down. Get these words out.* "I'm not...I'm not the girl of your fantasies." No way did someone like Jake fantasize about someone like her. She was boring. Quiet. The girl who'd never broken a single curfew back in high school.

Meanwhile, Jake had broken every rule that existed.

His lips twisted in a smile that never reached his eyes. "Harris has a big-ass mouth. One of his many flaws."

"Are the two of you friends?" True was trying to get a handle on their relationship.

"Something like that." He edged closer. "Used to hate the guy, to be honest. Thought he was an arrogant, know-it-all asshole. Now I tolerate him for football games and bowling nights. And because he can make one mean burger."

"That sounds like friendship."

"If it had been a real friendship, he would have told me that you were in danger." Hard. "Friends don't keep shit like that from friends."

Her heart was racing too fast. "Why would my danger matter so much to you?" Her fingers were lightly caressing his hand. She should stop that.

She didn't.

"Because you matter." Very low. Very deep. "Because Harris caught on to the fact that I've been fantasizing about you for a long time."

Jake Hale fantasizes about me. Me. And he's done it for a long time. "How did he catch on to that fact?" Breathless.

"Because if I saw you walking in town, I tended to lose my train of thought."

He could not have shocked her more. She was sure her mouth had just dropped open.

Jake rolled one shoulder in a shrug. "If you came into the coffee shop and I was there, I'd stop talking mid-conversation."

"I...don't remember seeing you in the coffee shop." Rosewood had one main shop that all the locals visited. It had been in operation for over fifty years. A centerpiece of town.

"You didn't see me because you always rushed in, all busy, grabbed your order, and headed straight out like you had a meeting to catch." A pause. "You didn't see me because I never approached you."

"Why not?"

He didn't speak.

"Jake?"

"I didn't think someone like you would want me." He tugged his hand free. "I'm going to poke around the museum. See if anything stands out to me. I'll talk to the guard you mentioned, Robert. And any other guards who might be here today."

Her hands twisted in front of her. She missed touching him.

He pointed at her as his jaw hardened. "Don't think of leaving the museum without me."

"I actually can't leave at all. Or at least, I can't leave for long." She would have to dash out and snag appropriate attire because... "We're hosting a Christmas event for the kids tonight." Something she should have mentioned to him sooner, but she'd been distracted by, oh, a dead body. "They're doing a holiday scavenger hunt in the permanent exhibit area. Then there will be caroling, hot cocoa, and Santa will make his grand appearance." The event had been her brainchild. All the proceeds were going to a local shelter for women and children.

His hand fell back to his side. "Sounds like fun."

She doubted he meant that. Not with the way he felt about Christmas. For him, there was no magic in the holiday. There never had been.

"If you're here, I'll be here," Jake added as he turned away.

Helpless, she took a step after him. "Jake!"

He looked back.

"Why wouldn't I want you?" She did want him. Hadn't she made that clear last night?

His powerful body stiffened. Then he spun to fully face her. "Because I'm a damn killer, True."

She froze to the spot.

"I've got blood on my hands. It will always be there. I

might have been fighting for my country, but people still died. I was *good* at what I did. Probably too good. And I still like hunting far too much. Why the hell do you think I have the job I do?" His mouth tightened. "And you don't want someone like that, do you? Not good, sweet, *kind* True Blakely. You will never really want someone like me."

"I—"

"True!" Aliyah Addams, the museum's marketing manager, burst into the exhibit room. "We have a problem. A major problem." The Christmas lights around her neck blinked on and off, the reindeer on her holiday sweater smiled, but her dark brown eyes were heavy with what could only be described as panic.

A problem? Is it as major as say...a dead body?

"Santa isn't coming," Aliyah announced starkly.

"Uh, yeah," Jake began. "Hate to give you a newsflash, but he never—"

True sent him a glare.

He stopped talking.

Her focus shifted back to Aliyah.

"He's got the flu. Can't be around the kids. All of the other Santas are already booked." Each word was filled with the same panic that gleamed in Aliyah's eyes. "Where are we going to find a Santa now? The night is going to be ruined!"

True's stomach twisted. Disaster was imminent.

"Wait a minute." Aliyah tapped her chin, and her gaze lasered on Jake. A broad smile spread across her face. "Hello, solution to our problem." A brief pause. "I don't think we've met."

"Uh, Aliyah, this is Jake Hale," True hurriedly made the introductions. "He's my—"

"Santa," Aliyah finished, voice triumphant.

"No." Jake shook his head. "Absolutely not."

True had intended to say...*He's my bounty hunter*. Or... *he's my bodyguard*. Or...*he's going to be my date...very, very soon*. She had not intended to call the man Santa. Never in a million years would she call him Santa.

But, apparently, Aliyah had other plans. She slowly walked around Jake, taking him in from all angles. "He'll need some padding around the middle. Got to hide those abs, but this can work. This can definitely work!"

"No." An adamant denial from True as she took up a protective position in front of Jake. "He's not a Christmas fan, Aliyah. He's not doing this." She would not put Jake in his own nightmare.

Aliyah frowned. "But we're desperate." She craned around True so she could better study Jake. "Did you *miss* the desperate part? Do you want True to be desperate?"

"I'm helping True with a case." Jake's rumbling reply. "I'm not putting on a big red suit and ho-ho-hoing my way through the night."

True glanced back at him. "We'll find someone else." She could figure this out. "It's fine. Really. Aliyah and I can call around town. There are other options."

"Uh, no, there aren't," Aliyah chimed in. "I've already called around. All the Santas are booked. Didn't you hear me when I said that before? It's the Saturday before Christmas. If you are a Santa, this is your busiest weekend. Most Santas were booked for this period months ago. With our guy calling in sick, we're about to have a ton of disappointed kids, and what is worse than a disappointed kid on Christmas? All sad eyes and trembling lips and—"

"Hell." A growl from Jake.

"It would be for the kids," Aliyah emphasized with a wiggle of her eyebrows. "Those sweet, wonderful kids."

"Fuck." Jake exhaled. "I'll do it."

True whipped around in shock. "Are you sure?"

He stared at her. A muscle jerked along his jaw. But Jake nodded.

She inched closer to him and put her hands on his chest. Then she whispered, "But you don't even like Christmas."

"Maybe it's growing on me."

Her lips parted.

"Or maybe I'm doing it for you." Low. Words meant just for her. "Not the kids."

Warmth spiraled through her. She leaned onto her toes because she could absolutely kiss the man right then.

Aliyah clapped. "Perfect! I'll get the suit, and you can try it on now. Showtime will be here before we know it." Her heels clattered away.

True didn't move. At first, she just kept staring into Jake's dark and deep eyes. Then she slowly smiled because she actually was figuring out a whole lot about him. And Jake might claim that he was big, bad, and dangerous. He might say he was the wrong kind of man for her to want. But for a wrong kind of man, Jake certainly had a heart of gold. "Thank you."

His eyes glinted with intent. "You're gonna owe me."

"I'll pay anything you want." Hadn't she made that offer before? When they'd been in his office, and he'd agreed to take her case without hesitation? The cops had turned her away. He hadn't.

Wrong kind of guy? No. He was right. Exactly what she needed. She hugged him tightly. "Thank you, Jake."

"Ho, fucking ho," he groused. "You tell *no one* about this, understand? No one. This is one of those secrets that you carry to the grave. And you are damn well not to tell Harris, understand? Especially not him. And not my assistant Perry, either. Jeez, not Perry. The kid would never let me hear the end of it. He'd suddenly be convinced that I was overflowing with Christmas spirit."

She beamed up at Jake.

He blinked at her. His voice roughened as he added, "And I will be collecting on what is owed to me." His gaze had just gone feral.

Please, please do collect. Collect all night long.

She could hardly wait.

"How about a down payment?" Had she really just said those husky words? Her attempt at flirtation? Seduction?

His widening eyes confirmed that she had, indeed, said them.

No time to take the words back. No time for hesitation. She curled her hands around his neck and hauled him toward her. Jake's mouth crashed onto hers. The kiss was a little clumsy because she was acting on nerves and need, but Jake took things over and turned the kiss from clumsy into...into...

Savage delight.

His tongue thrust into her mouth. He licked. He claimed. He had need coursing through her veins. A need that she only seemed to feel with him. Wildness rose within her. The good girl was so done. Being good for so long had gotten her nothing that she wanted.

An ex-husband who cheated.

A stalker who was trying to kill her.

A dead body.

Good was not working. Maybe it was time for something new.

His hands were on her waist. Her body pressed hard to Jake's, and there was no missing his arousal. He wanted her. She wanted him.

Take him. They didn't have to follow any rules. Jake probably still hated rules. He was a guy who lived on the edge, and she wanted to live there with him. A moan trembled from her, and he kissed her ever harder. His hands began to lift her up against him.

"Found it!" Aliyah called out happily. "Want to try on the Santa suit?"

Jake's head slowly lifted. He stared down at True. Her panting breath seemed far, far too loud.

Then his head lowered. Not for him to kiss her again. Instead, his mouth went toward her right ear. And he whispered, "What I want...is to fuck you."

I want you to fuck me, Jake.

"And I will. When we are alone again, you will be mine." She felt his tongue lick the edge of her ear. "Ready to get on the naughty list, True?"

Her whole body shuddered. *Yes, please.*

Chapter Six

"The naughty list is more fun. Prove me wrong."
– Jake Hale

"I know you're not Santa."

Jake raised an eyebrow at that statement. The cute kid currently sitting on his left knee couldn't see the small movement—not with the giant, white beard, fake bushy brows, and the huge red hat that dipped over his forehead.

"It's too close to Christmas." She nodded, and her serious eyes—a warm shade of gold—held his. "The real Santa is busy at the North Pole." Her voice lowered, "You're one of his spies."

How was he supposed to respond to those words? And since when did Santa have spies? Clueless, Jake remained silent.

"I know all about them." Another sage nod from her. She wore a bright red dress, and her black hair was twisted in a delicate bun on top of her head. "Santa sends out spies to find out what gifts the kids want. They report back to him. I mean, not like the man can really be here *and* at the mall on Fifth Street at the same time, am I right?"

He could not fault her logic.

"And the Santas you see everywhere—they all look different. Because they *are* different." She leaned toward him and lowered her voice even more before she whispered, "Spies."

Should he nod? Jake did, just in case.

"That's what I thought," she replied with satisfaction.

"Taneisha!" A stylish woman in a green turtleneck frowned at the girl. "Did you tell Santa what you'd like this year?" Her hair was cut short, and hoop earrings dangled from her small earlobes.

"Telling him!" Taneisha quickly called back. She licked her lips. "Here's the deal. *You* tell the real Santa. Tell him I got what I wanted. Mom's not sick any longer, and we're gonna be just fine."

Fuck. Jake's whole body tensed. His gaze cut back to the mom. The short hair...that was new hair growth. And the mom was a little too thin, as if she'd just lost a lot of weight. *Or been very, very sick.*

But the mom was smiling and taking photos of her daughter with her phone. Looking as happy as could possibly be. As if she didn't have a problem in the world. That was the thing about people. You never knew what weight others were carrying. He'd read once that some people made heavy loads look easy, but that was just a trick. People were always weighed down. You just might not know it.

Growing up, Tommy and I made sure no one ever knew

how bad things got after my dad left. And his mom? She'd worked so hard to keep their home going.

"Thanks for being a spy," the girl told him. Taneisha threw her arms around his neck. "And I hope you have a good Christmas, too." Then she was gone in a flash, running toward her mom. They walked away, holding hands.

He just stared after them. His breath came in and out, slowly. And his chest ached.

That is one hell of a kid.

Taneisha looked back and winked at him. Then she mouthed, "*Spy.*"

"Uh..." Aliyah cleared her throat as she crept from behind Santa's throne. Yeah, he had an actual throne for the last-minute gig. "Did my niece just call you a spy?" Aliyah asked.

She had. "That's your niece?"

"Yeah. And my sister, Maya, is the woman holding her hand."

He looked up at Aliyah and caught her blinking a few times as she stared after her family.

"She's doing better now." Low. "We all are." An exhale. "My sister saw the same doc that treated True's mom years ago. But Maya's cancer was caught sooner. We had a different result."

Sonofabitch. He remembered hearing that True's mom had died of cancer. True's father had passed away a year after that. Jake had been overseas at the time. And, shortly after her father's passing, True had married the prick in Atlanta.

Jake found himself looking for True. Needing to see her. Because, dammit, he hadn't even asked about her family. *I haven't asked enough about her.*

He'd just told True that he planned to fuck her.

How could she not be swept away by his charm?

I am such a dick.

Aliyah closed one hand over his shoulder. "Okay, now spill it while we have a moment."

Spill what?

"Maya gave me one mission. To find out what Taneisha just said she wanted for Christmas. The girl has been a vault all year, refusing to say anything. So I need the gift, and I need it now."

But Jake shook his head. "She has what she wants."

Aliyah frowned.

"She said her mom was better."

"Dammit." Aliyah swiped a hand across her cheek. "She *is* better. Maya kicked cancer's ass."

"Taneisha didn't want anything else." He peered across the room and found Taneisha hugging True. They were laughing about something. What was the kid? Seven? Eight?

A kid who believed in Christmas spies. "Got an idea," he said, voice a little gruff as he forced his stare back to Aliyah. "Buy her a spy set. Include a note that says she's now part of the team."

"What in the world are you talking about?" Aliyah stared at him as if he'd lost his mind.

Like that was new. People often gave him those types of looks.

"A spy set. You know, maybe some walkie talkies, a pair of binoculars, some undercover glasses to wear as a disguise." He nodded. "She will love it."

"You had better be right about this."

Oh, Jake thought that he was.

"More kids are waiting. You ready for them, Santa?"

Yeah, yeah, actually, he was. "Ho, ho, ho."

* * *

"I LIKE THE NEW BOYFRIEND," Aliyah announced when the last kid left the museum. She and True were at the museum's main doors. They'd been waving and thanking the attendees who filed out. "Wasn't sure at first, but he grew on me. The man is damn good with kids."

And that had been one major surprise. True had been stunned to see Jake getting the kids to laugh and chat freely with him during the event. "Everyone seemed happy, right?" she asked.

"Everyone was thrilled," Aliyah confirmed. "Total success. Now go and grab your hot Santa and ho, ho, ho up the rest of the night."

True felt a blush rise in her cheeks even though that was, ah, very much her plan.

"We clear to lock the entrance doors?"

She gave a little jerk at the question and turned to see Robert Moss standing at attention near the security desk. He'd been on duty that night. Robert always preferred the night shift. Keys jingled from his belt as he slowly ambled toward her. The light hit on his salt-and-pepper hair. He flashed his usual, warm smile.

"All clear," she agreed. "Thanks, Robert."

He bobbed his head. "Glad you're bringing some life back to this place."

"Me, too," Aliyah mumbled. "I swear, we were a breath away from shutting down, and then you came to town." She gave True a quick hug. "Have I told you how grateful I am for your divorce? That sounds horrible, doesn't it?" She tightened her hold. "But you're better off without the ex. And this town is better *with you here.*"

Not everyone in the town would agree. "Tell that to the dead man under my tree." She'd talked to Aliyah some about the horrible incident. Talking had been necessary after the story broke on the news.

Aliyah pulled back and studied True with worried eyes. "Hot Santa is working on that case, isn't he?"

True nodded.

"He's going to keep you safe." Not a question.

But, once more, True nodded. He was.

Robert secured the entrance doors. True and Aliyah would leave through the smaller, staff exit at the back, but first, she'd wait for Jake to get changed out of his Santa suit. *She'd* changed out of her yoga pants and sweatshirt earlier—a fast run to a department store with Jake had yielded a festive green dress and new heels for the holiday event. But she'd left her purse and phone in her office. She'd need to grab those items before meeting Jake. "I have to hit my office, then I'll be leaving with Jake." She pointed at Aliyah. "You have a wonderful night."

"You, too." Aliyah backed away and winked. "Something tells me your night might be way better than mine." A little wince. "Especially since I have to pick up some spy gear."

Spy gear?

But Aliyah tossed a wave and was gone.

Robert peered beyond the glass doors and out into the night.

The museum seemed so quiet. She definitely needed to hurry and find Jake. *After I snag my bag and phone.* "Good night, Robert."

"Night, True."

She hustled down the hallway, with her heels clicking. Her office was in the back near the Egyptian display. She felt herself tensing as she slipped in front of the double doors that led into the grand exhibit area. *This used to be my favorite part of the whole building. I loved that exhibit space.* She'd been so proud of it. Now the sight of those closed, double doors made her nervous.

True hurried into her office. She grabbed her purse and phone.

She frowned at the phone's screen. *One missed call.* From a number that should not be calling her.

Her ex's number. What in the world could Richard possibly want?

She shoved the phone into the small bag. She'd had the purse with her when she first went to Jake's office. It held a few very important necessities—like a small hair brush, lip stick, powder. In other words, her emergency supplies.

She turned out her lights, exited the office, and squared her shoulders as she once more hurried past the double doors that led to the Egyptian display.

Except...one of the doors was ajar.

True frowned. And stopped.

Because that wasn't right. She'd specifically locked the doors to the Egyptian display area before the museum's holiday event had started. She hadn't wanted anyone slipping inside by mistake.

But one door was definitely ajar now.

And that wasn't good.

The doors were closed when I went into my office. Weren't they? Had she looked closely enough before? Or had she been too focused on getting past the exhibit because it made her nervous?

She tiptoed toward the double doors. Her fingers

pushed against the open door, and it slid open a few more inches. "Hello?" Her head dipped inside.

A faint light glowed from within. Like...a flashlight? *No* lights should have been on inside that big space.

"This area isn't open yet," True explained as she took a few steps into the exhibit hall. Had a child wandered in by mistake? She'd thought that everyone had left, but maybe she'd been mistaken. *But I wasn't wrong about locking the doors. I know I locked them.* "Be sure and come back in the new year," True added quickly. "We'll be open then."

Crash.

She jumped. Something had just smashed into the floor. One of the replica vases she'd carefully arranged? The real vases were still in storage and wouldn't be brought out until after Christmas. True spun around and ran back for the doorway.

But someone grabbed her. A figure lurched from the darkness. And before she could scream, a hand slammed over her mouth.

* * *

"Where the hell is True?" Jake flattened his hands on the security desk at the front of the museum. "She wouldn't just leave without telling me."

The guard behind the desk—Robert Moss—frowned at Jake. "I told you already that True and Aliyah left earlier. True was getting her phone, and I think she said that she'd meet you outside." He made a shooing motion with his hands. "So go look outside. Near the back exit."

Another guard ambled toward them. Younger, fresh-faced, with close-cropped, dark hair. "The West Hallway is clear," he said. Braden Wallace. Jake had interviewed both guards earlier. They'd had zero useful intel to give him.

Braden was working his way through college—a psych major. He'd taken the security gig because he liked to study at night when the museum was quiet. And his days were left free to attend classes. Jake had gotten Perry to run a background check on everyone at the museum. Braden had come up clean.

So had Robert. A former Atlanta cop, the guy had retired to Rosewood only to get bored and had signed up for the security gig at the museum three years ago. He'd quickly been promoted to head of security.

The two guards who worked the day shift—Sydney Snow and Marc Chan—had both showed similarly clean records. Actually, all of the staff members at the museum were perfect on paper.

"The West Hallway." Jake cocked his head. "True's office is on that hallway." Her office and the Egyptian exhibit.

Braden nodded. "Yep. And Miss True's office was all shut down for the night. Lights off. Door closed." His brows beetled. "Is there a problem?"

Yeah, his gut said there was most definitely a problem. And it wasn't just the fact that he was still wearing his damn Santa suit. The problem was that True had vanished. "I looked out back. She wasn't near my ride." They'd come to the museum together. Not like she could leave without him.

"Maybe she decided to take off with Aliyah. They do that sometimes. Go out for drinks and ladies' night." Robert scratched his jaw. "Want me to call Aliyah or True for you?"

He'd already whipped out his phone. "On it." But he'd tried calling True a few moments before. No answer.

Then or…

Now.

Her voicemail picked up, and her warm voice told him, "This is True. So sorry I can't take your call. Leave me a message, and I'll get back with you as soon as I can. Thanks."

"True, where the hell are you?" Jake demanded as he began to head back toward the West Hallway. "Call me when you get this—"

The museum plunged into darkness.

Complete and total darkness.

"What in the hell?" he snarled even as he hung up the call.

"It's the breaker. We're an old place." Robert's voice drifted to him in the darkness.

Old was an understatement. They were in one of the few historic buildings left in town. As in…a building that had been there since the 1800s.

"Wiring is being updated with all the new security bells and whistles that True wants." The keys jingled from Robert's waist as he walked. "I'll reset things. Just took too much power—that happens with the light display outside. The reindeer and sleigh look great on the roof, but they make the power go off and on a few times a week. We're lucky this didn't happen when all the kids were here."

Lucky.

A flashlight turned on and hit Jake in the face. "Why don't you go wait outside?" Robert advised. "Don't want you getting lost in the dark."

Jake tapped on his phone's screen. The phone's light turned on instantly. Illumination just as strong as the glow coming from Robert's flashlight. "I'm good, and I'm not leaving without True." He turned and headed for the West Hallway.

"Told you, she's not in her office!" Braden called. He had a flashlight on, too. It shone behind Jake.

Jake kept walking. "I'm just going to check again."

Keys jingled and clanked behind him as Robert hurried to get the lights turned on. *The place loses power two or three times a week? Talk about your security nightmare. No wonder True wants the whole system upgraded ASAP.*

Jake kept his phone in his hand and used the light as a guide. Jake also dialed True one more time.

He stilled when he heard the faint hum of a phone ringing nearby.

His head turned to the left. He lifted up his light. Saw the closed double doors that led to the Egyptian display.

"This is True. So sorry I can't take your call..."

He hung up.

Then immediately dialed again.

Jake heard the faint hum of a ringing phone coming from inside the closed double doors. He grabbed for the doorknob on the right. Twisted it. *Locked.* Automatically, he twisted the left doorknob, too. Both were locked. But...

"This is True. So sorry I can't—"

Jake's phone was at his ear, being held in place by his shoulder.

True's phone was inside the Egyptian display area. Maybe she'd left it in there earlier. Or *maybe* True was in that space right the hell then. "True!" Jake bellowed.

No response.

"True!" He shoved his phone into one of the billowing pockets in the Santa coat.

Footsteps thundered toward him. His head turned, and

a flashlight hit him dead in the eyes. What the fuck was up with these security bozos shining their lights at him?

"What's happening?" Braden demanded.

"Unlock these doors, now," Jake fired.

"I-I don't have the key to this display space. I don't get access to the big exhibit areas. I mostly patrol the exterior and the open hallways. Robert has keys for the high-value rooms. We can go find him—"

Screw that. Jake lifted his big, black, Santa boot...and he kicked in the doors.

Chapter Seven

"Santa Claus is coming to town.
And he is gonna kick the ass of anyone who wants to hurt True." – Jake Hale

"What are you doing?" A desperate shriek from Braden. "You can't—"

The lights flashed on overhead even as Jake bounded inside the exhibit. His gaze cut around the exhibit space. No sign of True. But there were some broken shards of pottery near a black display stand.

"She's not here," Braden said, voice cracking a bit around the edges. "And you just broke the doors. I am going to be in so much trouble. We have to get out of here, now."

Jake hauled his phone back out and dialed her number again. It rang once, twice—he heard the rings in that damn display room. His focus zeroed in on the sarcophagus to the right.

"This is True. So sorry I can't—

Jake thrust the phone back into a pocket and lunged for the sarcophagus. He could hear rings coming from inside that sarcophagus and...faint thumping sounds.

"No!" Braden jumped in front of him. "Don't smash it the way you smashed the doors. This is on loan! Miss True will kill me if you damage it! Kill. Me!"

"Get the fuck out of the way, or I may damage you, kid."

The kid got the fuck out of the way. Jake shoved aside the top of the sarcophagus. Shouldn't the thing have been secured more? Locked in place or something?

Only when that top slid to the side, he didn't see some ancient mummy waiting for him. He saw True. With ropes on her hands and feet and some kind of gag in her mouth. Her eyes were wide and terrified, and a killing fury tore through him even as he hauled her out of the sarcophagus. *A freaking coffin. Someone stuffed True in a coffin.*

"Sweets?" With True in his arms, Jake double-timed it out of the exhibit area even as Braden trailed him.

The kid kept saying, "OhmyGod" over and over again.

Once clear of that cursed display room, Jake lowered True to her feet. He ripped away the gag. Tore off the ropes that bound her wrists and ankles.

When she was free, True threw herself against him. Her small purse banged into his side. Her purse—the purse that must have her *phone* inside it. His arms closed around her.

"I was afraid you wouldn't find me." She shuddered and clutched him even tighter. "I could barely move. I was freaking out, and I thought you wouldn't *find me.*"

Oh, the fuck, no. The killing rage just flared hotter within him. "Baby, I'd find you in hell, then I'd beat the shit out of the devil who took you there." Over her shoulder, he glared at a gaping Braden. "Call the cops, *now.*"

Braden yanked out his phone. He called the cops, and Jake held True as tightly as he could.

"Don't leave me," True pleaded.

Rage twisted within him. "I'm not going anywhere." His fear was too raw. His rage too savage. Someone would pay for terrorizing her. Jake would make certain of that fact.

You've just fucked with the wrong Santa.

* * *

Harris ran his index finger along the bridge of his nose as he studied Jake. "Santa, huh?"

"Fuck yourself."

"Is this a new fashion choice, were you hit hard by the holiday spirit, or were you—"

"I did it for True." A True who was currently sitting at the desk in her office, with her shoulders hunched, and her beautiful eyes darkened by far too many shadows. Jake stood right beside her, and he found himself touching her every few moments.

Running his knuckles over her cheek.

Holding her hand.

Squeezing her shoulder.

Wanting to pull her into my arms and run the hell out of here with her.

But first, he had to deal with the cops. Or rather, one cop in particular. A currently annoying Harris.

"Can we get back to the freaking *crime?*" Jake snapped. "Or do you just want to ride my ass about the Santa suit all night?" He still had on the suit, so sue him. At least he'd ditched all the extra padding—it was in the chair to the right. He hadn't left True alone for a moment. Would not leave her. So he'd just be leaving that museum with the big red coat on.

Harris's gaze darted over to True. "You're *sure* you never saw your attacker?"

She swallowed. "It was dark when I went inside the exhibit area. N-not totally dark. It should have been. The door was ajar—that shouldn't have been the case, either. I *locked* the exhibit before the holiday event so no guests would wander inside. But someone got in." Her words came faster. "Someone had a light on inside. A small light—like a flashlight. And that someone—" Her breath panted out. "He put a hand over my mouth before I could scream. Everything happened so fast. I tried to fight, but he threw me in the sarcophagus." A shudder swept over her. "I tried to punch him, but he tied my hands. My feet. It was *so fast.* He was too strong. And then he sealed me up." Another shudder. "He sealed me up," True repeated, seeming dazed.

Shock.

Jake turned her chair toward him. Then he dropped to his knees in front of True so she had to stare straight at him. "Hey, sweets." His voice was soft. Gentle. For her. "I want you to focus on me."

She stared straight at him.

"Pull in a deep breath for me," he urged her.

She did.

"Let it out."

She slowly exhaled.

He nodded. "You're not sealed up."

True shook her head. Her dark hair slid over her shoulder.

"You will *never* be sealed up again. We're going to find him, and I swear to you, he will pay."

"Uh, Jake?" Harris tapped him on the shoulder. "Can we have a word, outside?"

"No." Just that. No.

"What?" Harris seemed to have trouble understanding Jake's response.

"I'm not leaving True. You want a word, then we have it right here." His hand rose, and his knuckles skimmed down her cheek again. He just had to keep touching her.

Her head turned into his touch. "I want to go home."

Her home was a crime scene. They'd go to his place. *Home.* Jake rose. He reached for her hand.

"Who had keys to the display room?" Harris asked. "The lock is shattered to hell and back now—because of Jake's kick to the door—but the guard, Braden, he said the lock appeared undisturbed when he and Jake first arrived. That tells me that maybe the perp who got inside had a key."

"Robert has a key," Jake told him. "He's the head security guard. Braden told me that Robert had one."

"And I have one." True had risen to her feet. Her right hand remained twined with Jake's. Her left hand opened the top desk drawer. A key ring—one much smaller than the massive ring that hung from Robert's belt—waited inside. "My keys are *always* in the top drawer." She reached for her keys.

But Jake's fingers closed around her hand. "How about we let Harris and his crew dust for prints on those? Just in case the creep took your keys so he could access the display room and then he put them back in the drawer. If he did that, maybe the asshole left prints behind."

A jerky nod from True. She let Jake ease her around the desk and toward the door. But she paused near a watchful Harris. "He had on gloves. When he put his hand over my mouth, I-I felt them." Her gaze darted back to her desk. "If he was wearing gloves, then there will be no prints."

"We'll check. Thoroughly," Harris added. No signs of his earlier humor showed on his face. In fact, the faint lines near his mouth appeared extra grim. "You remember anything else? Anything the perp said?"

"He didn't speak."

"What about a smell? You notice any smells?"

A negative shake of her head.

"You said he was strong." Harris was clearly not giving up on getting some kind of description for the perp. "You get an idea of how tall he was?"

Another shake of her head. "I'm sorry. I was so scared, and...I wish I could help more. He was strong enough to pick me up. To shove me inside the sarcophagus."

"Good thing a mummy wasn't in there." This time, Harris was the one to shudder. "Talk about hell."

True stiffened. "Yes, that would have been hell." Her head turned toward Jake. "May we go home now? Please?"

Damn straight they could. He took a step forward even as he tightened his grip on True's hand.

But Harris stepped into his path. "The museum was wide open to the town tonight. That's a whole lot of suspects—and I'm not just talking about the registered attendees at the event. *Anyone* could have come inside."

Jake knew they had a list of suspects that would stretch for a mile.

"She was gagged. Bound." Worry darkened Harris's voice as he finished, "Whoever did this isn't playing."

Like Jake needed to be told that. Dead bodies weren't dumped for shits and giggles.

"You don't want to talk privately, so I'll just have to put this out there for her to hear." Harris's lips tightened. "True,

I think the plan was to hide you until Jake—and anyone else still here after your holiday event—left the facility. Then I think the perp was going to finish you off."

All the color—and there hadn't been much there—drained from True's face. She swayed.

Dammit.

"I can offer you police protection," Harris continued determinedly. "I can move you into a safe house. I can—"

"No." This time, True's fingers tightened around Jake's. "I have protection—I have Jake. I'm safe as long as I'm with him."

Harris shared a long look with Jake. "You got this?"

Oh, he did. "If the bastard comes at her again, he's dead." Did that count as having it? Jake thought it did.

Harris's eyes widened. "You can't say that to a cop!"

Jake shrugged. He'd just said it, hadn't he? No stutter. Loud and clear.

"And you're in a jolly Santa suit!" Harris huffed. "You can't make threats when you're dressed like—"

"Ho, ho, ho," Jake growled. "If he comes at her again, I'll deck the bastard's halls so hard that he will never move again. Better? Is that Christmasy enough for you?"

"No, no, that is *not* better!" Harris's eyes were huge. "You need to leave this to the police—to *me!*"

"Then the police need to get busy. Because there is no way in the world that I'm letting him get True again." He pulled her closer to him even as he told Harris, "If you need us, we'll be at my place." For the rest of the night. But come morning, they were hunting. The bastard was not getting away with what he'd done to True.

Harris looked pissed, but he didn't argue.

"There's...one more thing," True said, hesitant. "I'm sure it's nothing, but..."

Both men focused on her.

"Right before I noticed that the exhibit door was open, I realized that I'd missed a call from my ex-husband."

Jake stiffened. The ex. From Atlanta.

Where the dead man under the tree just happened to live and work...Like it wasn't easy to connect those dots.

"Richard and I haven't talked in ages. There's no reason for him to call me, and—it's odd, right?" A little furrow appeared between True's brows. "The dead man in my home was from Atlanta."

She'd clearly been connecting the dots, too.

"Richard—Richard Wells—is a prosecutor in Atlanta. He might have known the man we found in my house. I don't—I don't think Richard would hurt me." She squeezed her eyes shut. "Forget it. I'm just making crazy connections."

Jake didn't think there was anything crazy about her at all.

When Harris dipped his head, Jake understood the detective felt the same way. "On it," Harris murmured.

Jake was going to be *on it,* too.

True's eyes opened. "Do you have any other questions? Can we leave?"

"No more questions. Not for now, anyway." Harris inclined his head. "But if you see anything or anyone suspicious, you call me, got it?"

If Jake saw anyone suspicious, he was taking the prick down. He pulled True closer to his body and, together, they headed into the museum's hallway. Uniformed cops were in the Egyptian display room. Braden and Robert were talking quietly to one police officer. They didn't even seem to notice when Jake and True slipped away.

But as soon as Jake had gotten True out of the building...

"Boss!" Perry rushed toward them. Light snow flurries danced in the air around him, and a puff of icy fog appeared before his mouth. "I got your text. The cops wouldn't let me in, so I just waited out here for you." His anxious stare darted to True as the nearby parking lot light fell on them. "You okay, ma'am?"

She shivered.

Jake shouldered out of his Santa coat and put it around her shoulders.

"Is that a Santa coat?" Perry squinted.

"You're always giving me your coats to wear," True murmured. "That's...kind of you."

He didn't feel particularly kind. He felt like ripping apart the bastard who'd terrorized her and then sealing that prick in a coffin. *Let's see how that feels, asshole.*

No, he'd never been kind. That had been her. True was the one who volunteered at the local soup kitchen at Thanksgiving. She was the one who organized the Christmas toy drive—yes, he'd donated when he saw her putting up flyers around town. She was the one who did things to help other people.

He was the bastard. The one who hunted down criminals for money. The one who got a sick rush from the job because he was a predator straight to his core.

She should be running far away from him.

I will not let her go.

"Uh, boss?" Perry was back to squinting at him. "You said you needed me for some work?"

Actually, he had quite the to-do list for his assistant. "Find Richard Wells."

True's head swung toward him. "My ex? You want Perry to find him?"

Damn straight, he did. Jake nodded grimly even as he focused on his assistant. "I want to know exactly where the guy was tonight. And yesterday, for that matter. I also want to know what connection he may have to Dylan Dunn."

Perry straightened. "This is my first big case, isn't it?"

"Perry, don't you disappoint me."

"I would *never.*" Passionate. The kid looked like he was fighting the urge to salute. The ski cap on his head bobbed with his eagerness. "On it. Anything else?"

Perry was good with computers. Far better than just *good,* actually. One of the reasons Jake had finally given in and hired Perry had been because of the kid's tech skills. "Check the financials of the employees at the museum. I want to know if anyone has seen a recent influx of cash." The background checks on the employees had turned up clean, but Jake needed a deep and dirty dive into their financial records.

True sucked in a sharp breath. "On everyone? Even Aliyah?"

"Everyone." They had to be thorough. "Let me know if any red flags fly, particularly on Braden Wallace and Robert Moss."

Perry nodded. "I swear, I will not disappoint you."

"Great. Fabulous. I know you won't."

"And may I say, sir, how happy I am to see that you've gotten into the holiday spirit—"

"No, Perry, don't say that shit. Just get to work."

Perry all but ran away. His red scarf billowed behind him.

The snow flurries fell a little harder.

"I'd already decided to investigate your ex even before I

found out about the phone call," he told True as they made their way to his SUV. He opened her door. Lifted her into the seat. Not that she needed lifting.

Another excuse to touch her.

Jake didn't immediately shut the passenger door. Instead, he leaned in toward her. "I'm going to investigate *anyone* that I think is a danger to you. You aren't going to be threatened again. That shit is stopping."

She pulled the red Santa coat closer to her body.

His chest ached. She'd just wanted a good night. Wanted to make the kids happy. He'd seen her working tirelessly. Preparing the hot chocolate. Giving out brightly decorated packages—a gift for each kid. The event had been free, he knew that. He also knew she'd had to spend hours and hours getting all the decorations just right. The place had been perfect. A Christmas dream. And she'd been *happy*. Her smile had lit the room. He'd been distracted by it more than once.

More than once? Try over and over again.

But she wasn't smiling any longer. She was too tense. Too pale. Too scared.

He hated that. "How can I make it better?" Gruff.

She blinked. No answer came from True. Right. Because he couldn't make it better. Not yet.

It will be better when I catch this bastard and throw him into a cage.

"Put on your seatbelt, sweets," he urged her. "We'll be home before you know it." He shut the door. Double-timed it around the SUV. He climbed in the driver's side. Cranked the vehicle, and started to shift the ride into reverse.

Her fingers touched the back of his hand. "Make love to me."

Christmas music blared in the vehicle. He *swore* that he

hadn't put it on holiday music, but at this time of the year, all the stations were pretty much playing Christmas music non-stop. And because of the loud music, Jake could not be sure that he'd actually heard True say what he *hoped* she'd said.

She pulled her hand back.

He turned down the radio. Then his head swung toward her. "Say that again."

She bit her lower lip.

"True?" *Say it again. I need to hear those words again.*

"You asked how you could make it better."

His heart slammed into his chest.

"Will you make love to me?" She seemed to hold her breath.

No, dammit, he was the one holding his breath because holy shit, was this real? *True wants me to make love to her? Now?*

"I shouldn't have asked—forget it," she rushed to say. "I'm not myself. I just—"

He leaned forward. Caught her chin with his fingers. And kissed her. Soft. Careful. Because she deserved every care in the world. "I will make it so better," he vowed against her mouth, "that you will be screaming for more."

Chapter Eight

"Oh, I can jingle all the way, all night long."
– Jake Hale

I WILL MAKE IT SO BETTER THAT YOU WILL BE SCREAMING for more.

Somehow, Jake had arranged for her clothes and toiletries to be brought to his place. Maybe his assistant, Perry, had brought them over while they'd been at the museum? However the magic had happened, True was extremely grateful. When she exited the shower—feeling semi-normal once again—she slid into the blue silk pajamas that waited for her.

Then she kind of froze in the bedroom because...

How exactly did she go about collecting on Jake's promise? Did she just walk up to the man, stare into his deep, dark eyes and say something like, *"I'm ready to scream now, please."*

Yes, so, that didn't feel right. Felt far too bold for her.

Far too out of her comfort zone. But everything she was doing with Jake was beyond her comfort zone. Maybe that was a good thing.

She crept toward the bedroom door. She'd rushed down the hallway and into the bedroom after they arrived. He'd stayed in the den. And...

Just go find the man. Kiss him. You don't have to say a word.

Her hand curled around the doorknob. She yanked the door open, and, not giving herself time to think any longer or hesitate, she hurried toward the den. Only when she was halfway to her goal, True paused because she was sure she heard the sound of...Christmas music? In Jake's home?

With slower steps, she continued on her mission. True followed the music into the den. Flames flickered and danced in the fireplace. Two glasses of wine waited on the coffee table, and, as soft, instrumental Christmas music played in the air, Jake stood with his back to her. He seemed to be focusing very, very hard on the dancing flames.

"Feel better?" he asked without looking back.

She jumped at the rumble of his voice. *Settle down.* Ha. That was an impossibility. "Well, I no longer feel like I'm trapped in a three-thousand-year-old coffin, so there's that." Though she was sure a new fear had been unlocked that would haunt her forever. *Hello, claustrophobia.* "I didn't thank you, earlier. I should have." Apparently, talking was necessary. No running straight to the man and kissing him as if her life depended on it.

"You don't need to thank me for anything." He kept staring at the fire.

"You saved my life." She took one quick step toward him. "That's definitely worth a thank you."

His hand lifted and curled around the mantel. As she

stared at him, his grip tightened. "I've never been the good guy."

Another step. "Um, did you miss the part where you saved me? That definitely counts as good. Hate to break it to you, but I suspect your naughty streak is over. I think you're making the nice list for sure this year." Why was she trying to joke?

He looked over his shoulder at her. "You have no idea what I want to do to you."

Say again? Her feet became rooted to the spot. *Tell me. Tell me everything.*

"I'll never be on the *nice* list, sweets. Never in a million years. And the things running through my mind...the way I want to make you come screaming for me..." A shake of his head. "Not nice."

Her heartbeat raced in her chest. It had raced when she'd been trapped in the sarcophagus, but fear had fueled her during those horrible moments. She wasn't afraid now. Quite the opposite.

His dark eyes glittered. "Are you fucking me because you're grateful?" Low. Dark. Dangerous.

Her arms wrapped around her body. "I actually don't think we're fucking yet."

He whirled toward her. "We're about to be. And I want to know...*why.*" A demand.

He'd ditched the rest of the Santa suit. He wore a black t-shirt that stretched across his powerful chest. Jeans that hung low on his hips. His hair was disheveled. His eyes intense. And he was—far and away—the sexiest man she'd ever seen in her life.

Okay, not on the nice list. That wasn't the worst thing in the world. In fact...

Let me be on the naughty list with you.

"I want you," True blurted. Did that cover the *why* part of the equation well enough for him?

Jake stalked toward her. His movements were so predatory that she almost retreated. At the last moment, True held her ground and lifted her chin.

"I thought I'd take you, and just be grateful to finally have my fantasy." He stopped right in front of her. "But I want more."

"You can have everything." A whisper. Oh, damn. She probably shouldn't have said that. Did she look too eager? She felt too eager. But the thing was...

A woman could get a whole lot of perspective on life when she was suddenly trapped in an ancient coffin. *In my own hell.* She could realize that playing by the rules just got you a broken heart and broken dreams. She could realize that *maybe* you should reach out for what you wanted. Take it. Enjoy the wild ride.

His hand rose. Then, before he touched her, that hand fisted and fell back to his side. Disappointment rolled through her.

Jake shook his head. "I can't take advantage when you're scared out of your mind."

Was that what he thought he was doing? Taking advantage?

"I tried to set the scene." His gaze darted around the room. "Got you wine. Played music I thought you'd like."

Warmth spread inside of her. "The music is nice."

"But you don't...you don't want to cross this line with me. Hell, last night, you were saying we were going to date. Date, not fuck. You're scared now and you're acting out, and I don't want you hating me tomorrow."

She couldn't hate him. Utter impossibility.

"You're safe." His gaze came back to her. "And for once, I will not be the bastard the world thinks I am."

So he was rejecting her? And looking all stoic about it, as if he'd just made some major sacrifice? What did the man want, a cookie for turning her down?

Not happening. "You made a promise."

"I *will* keep you safe."

"Not talking about that promise. I'm talking about how I'd scream because things would be so good." She yanked up her pajama shirt and tossed it behind her. She hadn't put on a bra, and she stood there, with her nipples getting a wee bit cold and pebbling.

His gaze fell to her chest. "*True*."

"Everyone has always gone on and on about how good I am. Sounds boring as hell, frankly." She shoved down her pajama shorts—and her panties—and kicked them away. "And, honestly, can't someone be nice *and* naughty at the same time? Because I think it is possible."

"You're naked." Savage.

"Thank you for noticing." She was naked and nervous, but she would not back down. This was too important. He was too important. "I think you want me." Her gaze dropped to the front of his jeans. She swallowed. "You definitely want me."

"*True*."

"And I want you. When I was trapped, do you know what I thought?"

His gaze rose to her face. And, again, she almost retreated. No one had ever looked at her with such burning lust before.

But she stood her ground. Her naked ground. "I thought...*I wish I'd been with Jake last night*. I wish I had more than just fantasies of him. I wish I hadn't been scared for so long and that I'd just taken what I wanted."

Both of his hands were tight fists at his sides. "I'm *trying to be good,*" he gritted out.

"I don't want that. I want the man who promised me that I'd scream for him." A quick breath. "See, I've never done that for a man. Never come so hard that I screamed. But I have very, very high hopes for you. With you. I—"

His hands weren't at his sides any longer. They were on her. His mouth was on hers. He was pulling her against him, her body flush against his, and she kissed him with all the passion she had.

No fear.

No doubt.

Just lust.

Make me scream. Make me.

His hands tightened on her waist, and he lifted her up against him. She gasped, and the sound was swallowed by his mouth. He carried her a few steps, then he lowered her down onto the lush rug near the fire. Jake knelt beside her, still fully dressed, and the flames sent shadows—then light—chasing over his body. "You never screamed for the ex-husband?"

She shook her head.

"Never screamed for anyone?"

Another negative shake.

"You will for me."

Then he settled between her legs.

"Jake, I—"

His fingers went straight to her core. She was tense and way too nervous, and she flinched.

"Trust me," he breathed.

Then he lowered his head. His mouth—it went...

On her.

"Jake!" Her hands flew out. Up. All around as they grabbed for the rug and held on tightly.

His tongue dipped into her. His fingers teased her clit. Her hips shot eagerly toward him.

She'd, ah, thought they might work up to this part. Slowly. Like, start with kisses. Some touches. Then they'd get to—

He strummed her clit relentlessly, and a desperate moan broke from her. Then his mouth replaced his fingers on her clit. He licked her. Again and again and again, and her head thrashed against the rug. Her hips strained against him. He'd locked his hands around her waist so that he could easily force her closer to his mouth. There was no retreat. There was just need and pleasure.

Her eyes flew open. She didn't remember squeezing them shut. She looked down and saw Jake *going down* on her. Lapping her up like she was the best thing that he'd ever tasted in his entire life. The rest of the world didn't matter. Nothing mattered but this moment.

One of his long, strong fingers was inside her. He pushed another in. Stretched her. And lapped at her clit as she—*came.* True came on a sudden orgasm so powerful and sharp that there was no way she could hold back the cry that burst from her lips.

A scream. For him.

He kept his promise.

Jake kept licking her. Feasting. Driving her wild as she trembled and broke beneath him. When the climax finally eased, when the aftershock pulses still shook her core but she could actually think coherently again, Jake slowly raised his head.

"Always knew you'd taste that sweet." He licked his lips. "New favorite treat."

Her body was lax. Replete. The orgasm had rocked straight through her. It had obliterated her.

"Now I think you're ready."

He hauled his shirt over his head. Threw it across the room. The shadows and light rippled over his chest. She reached for him instantly.

His hands shoved down on either side of her head. "I want to be gentle with you."

He *had* been gentle.

"But I've been holding onto this need for a long time. Once I get in you..." His jaw hardened. "If I get too rough, if I do *anything* that makes you uncomfortable, you tell me."

He wasn't going to do anything she didn't want. "You need to get the jeans off." They were in the way. Her hand flew down as she tried to open the snap.

His fingers immediately covered hers. "I'm not like your other lovers, sweets."

"All two of them?"

His hand tightened on hers. "I will *own* you."

What did that even mean? "Do I get to own you, too?"

"You already do." A growl. "You need a safe word with me. It's been too long for you. I'm too big. And I *don't want you hurt.*"

"No, I don't think that's necessary—"

"You say the word if anything hurts you. *Pick* something, now."

Couldn't she just say...*Go slower?* Was that not happening? Fine, fine...anything to get the man's jeans off. "Sleigh bells."

He blinked.

"Sleigh bells if you need to slow down." Her breath

shuddered out. She wasn't worried about him slowing down. She needed the man to speed the heck up. "And jingle for when you need to go harder." She kissed him on the neck. Bit lightly. "Faster. *Jingle.*"

He pulled away.

She was the one blinking in confusion. But he just ditched his jeans and boxers.

Oh, wow. He was certainly built along way bigger lines than her ex. So, okay, yep, maybe she would need that *sleigh bells* bit if things got uncomfortable because he was absolutely going to wreck her if he wasn't careful.

He shoved on a condom that he'd hauled from his wallet, and Jake pushed her thighs apart as he came back to her. "Don't be afraid of me."

She hadn't been. Until she'd seen the full size of his dick. "Uh..."

The tip of his cock pushed into her. True couldn't help tensing.

His eyes remained locked on hers. "You're going to take me, and you're going to tell me if *anything* hurts."

A nod. Her hands reached for his shoulders.

His hand slid between their bodies. Worked her clit and a fast spasm of pleasure shot through her. Oh, yes, she liked that. The nervous tension transformed into fast need. *Jingle. Jingle. Jingle!*

He kissed his way down her neck, stopping to drop little bites along the way. His mouth felt incredible. Who would have known that her neck was so sensitive? It hadn't been before. But, honestly, with Jake, every part of her body felt hyperaware and sensitive. Primed.

She needed *more.*

"Jingle!" True called out.

His head shot up.

"That was the one that meant more. Faster. Harder." She squirmed beneath him. "I want more, Jake. I want everything." She wanted him fully in her.

But he went back to kissing her, to feathering his mouth over her as he slowly moved his head down. He continued to just have the broad tip of his dick inside of her. Finally, his mouth took her breast. Her body shivered as need cascaded through her. He licked and sucked her nipple and had her thrashing beneath him. But he didn't thrust deep into her. Why not?

Was he torturing her? This felt like torture. Her legs locked around his hips as she tried to take more of him inside of her. She wanted *more.* "Jake, please!"

He drove into her.

He stretched every single inch of her. For a moment, she was caught between pleasure and pain because his size was no joke. He'd warned her. She probably should have paid more attention.

He stilled. Rose up. Stared into her eyes.

Sleigh bells. That was what she was supposed to say if it was too much.

She clamped her lips together.

His fingers went to her clit. Rubbed. *Rubbed.* Her body unlocked for him. Desire spiraled.

Her head tipped back. He withdrew. Plunged into her. Withdrew. When he plunged deep once more, her hips slammed up to meet him. The rhythm became savage. Brutal. Absolutely beyond everything she'd known before. This wasn't some tame lovemaking. Some quick thrusts in the dark.

She grabbed for his shoulders. Held on tight. "Jingle," she whispered.

He growled. His hands slid beneath her. Curled around

her ass as he lifted her up against him so that Jake could thrust relentlessly. Her climax ripped straight through True as her nails raked over his skin. Once more, she screamed for him.

And he seemed to let go of his control. A snarl broke from him. His thrusts pistoned against her in a fast fury. His hands skimmed over her body. Seeming to touch—no, to brand and mark every single inch of her. His mouth was on her throat. Pressing. Licking. Biting. Her core spasmed around him as aftershocks from her climax pulsed through her. Sweat slickened their bodies as they tangled before the fire, and she didn't care.

This was perfect.

This was passion.

This was—

He stiffened against her. Slammed hard once more. Then he roared her name.

* * *

HE'D PLANNED to fuck her in a bed. Like a normal person. Like a *gentleman.* In a soft bed. Not on the hard floor of his den. Shit. There had been *steps* involved in his master plan.

Step one—get the fireplace going. Step two—turn on the Christmas music that he knew True loved. Step three—give her a glass of the wine she'd enjoyed the night before. Step four—talk to her. Charm her. He could be charming, dammit. Then he'd planned to take her into his bedroom. To not rush her.

To not fuck her on the floor.

His hands shoved against the rug as he heaved up. He'd been keeping his body off hers because he hadn't wanted to crush True with his weight. She shivered beneath him, and her long lashes lifted as she opened her eyes and stared at him.

She didn't say a word.

But she screamed for me earlier. Just as he'd wanted. She'd screamed twice. Because she'd come twice. And she'd raked her nails down his body. She'd left marks on him.

And he'd left marks on her. His gaze dropped to her neck. He could see the faint redness from his mouth.

She still hadn't spoken.

He should say something. *Or get her sweet ass off the floor, you jerk.* Yeah, yeah, that was what he should do. And he needed to do that fast because his eager dick was getting hard for her again. As if he hadn't just exploded inside of her and lost his ever-loving mind.

Clenching his back teeth, he began to withdraw. *Fuck but she feels good.* His own paradise. "True, I'm sorry that I—"

"That was amazing."

He blinked.

She smiled. The warm smile that reached her eyes and made his chest feel funny. Her hand reached up and her fingers skimmed down his cheek. "Can we do that again?"

Jake felt a big smile curve his own lips. "All night long." But first he had to ditch the condom. There were more condoms, though. In his bedroom. Where his *bed* was. Because he would not be taking her on the floor again. He could be civilized.

Maybe. Possibly. Potentially?

With True, his best-laid plans tended to get shot to hell and back.

He withdrew. Ditched the condom in the trash, then returned to her. True had sat up before the fireplace, and her head tilted back as he approached. As he stared at her, he stumbled. Jake never stumbled.

But this time, he did.

The fire was behind her, flickering and dancing, and True—naked True, his absolute dream—stared back at him with a warm, sweet smile on her face. A smile for him. She wanted him. She was happy and naked and waiting for him.

Who said Christmas miracles didn't happen?

Her smile flickered. "Jake?" She rose to her feet. Her beautiful breasts did a little jiggle that made his dick salute. "Is everything all right?"

He closed the distance between them. Stared down at her. "No."

Her brows rose.

"I'm not inside of you." His hand slid down her body. Moved between her legs.

She sucked in a quick breath and rose onto her toes. Her hands clamped around his arms as she steadied herself against him.

"I don't feel this tight, hot heaven squeezing my dick." But she was squeezing his fingers. "And I need my dick to be *in you* right now." He needed her climaxing around his cock. Shuddering and bucking as she went wild for him. "You going to take me again?"

Her hands tightened on him even as her cute little tongue snaked out to lick across her lower lip. "Thought we already agreed..."

His thumb brushed over her clit.

She gasped, then finished, "All...night long?"

One night wasn't going to cut it. Not for him. But it was probably better not to scare her and tell her that truth. Not yet. So they'd *start* with a night. His hand pulled away from the sweet heat he craved.

"Jake?"

He scooped her into his arms. Carried her down the hallway. Kissed her. And didn't let her go, not until he had her exactly where he wanted her.

In his bed.

Where I want her to stay.

Where he would make her come, again and again, as she screamed for him.

Jingle all night long.

Chapter Nine

"Do I have a favorite Christmas song? Oh, absolutely. 'Jingle Bells.'"
– True Blakely (and seconded by Jake Hale)

"JAKE! JAKE, HELP ME!"

Her scream woke him. Jake bolted up in bed, then he jumped *out* of the bed. Disoriented, he searched the darkness for danger.

Only none was there.

"Jake!" True thrashed in the bed.

He realized that she was having a nightmare, and in that nightmare, she was calling for him. "True." Soft. As gentle as he could be. He turned on the bedside lamp. The nearby clock showed it was four-thirty-one a.m. They'd only fallen asleep a short while ago.

I couldn't get enough of her. I wanted to fuck her endlessly.

But he'd finally pulled back.

Only for her to slip into a nightmare.

His hand closed around her shoulder. "Sweets, wake up."

"Jake!" That cry was still from her nightmare. Her eyes hadn't opened.

"I'm right here." *I'll always be here.* He shook her, lightly. "True, it's okay. You're safe. You're—" *With me.*

Her eyes flew open. Her breath heaved out. Trembles shook her whole body.

"It's okay," he repeated. "You were having a nightmare."

A tear leaked down her left cheek. "I was back...at the museum."

His teeth ground together. He'd feared as much.

"It was so dark in the sarcophagus. I couldn't get out. The rope was cutting into my wrists..."

He grabbed her left wrist. There was a faint bruise around her wrist from the rope. Around *both* of her wrists. As he sat on the bed beside her, Jake brought her left wrist to his mouth and gently kissed the tender skin. *I am going to find the sonofabitch, and he will pay.*

"In the dream, the lid was lifted, but...but it wasn't you standing there. It was a man in a ski mask."

The dead bastard at her house had come carrying a ski mask.

"I knew he was going to kill me."

His mouth pressed to her wrist once more. He could feel the frantic flutter of her pulse racing beneath his lips. "No one is going to kill you." But he would kill in an instant in order to keep her safe.

Whoops. Was he being too savage again? Screw that. He'd always been savage. Sometimes, a little savagery was exactly what you needed.

"Why is this happening?" Another tear slid down her cheek.

"I don't know. But we will find the bastard." Those tears of hers had to stop. They made his guts twist. Made him want to punch walls. Rip bastards apart. "Do you trust me?" The stark question spilled from him.

Hell. Why'd you ask her that? Of course, she doesn't trust you. You've been back in her world for some of the most dangerous moments of her life and she—

"Yes." No hesitation. "I do. You're the only one who believed me. You're the only one who helped me. Right from the start, you wanted to protect me."

Unease had him stiffening. "Don't make me out to be a hero." Because right from the start, he'd wanted to fuck her. By taking her case, he'd known that he'd have the opportunity to get close to True.

And she's in my bed. I have her where I've always wanted her.

The new problem? He never wanted to let her go.

But heroes didn't take cases because they wanted to fuck the women they were supposed to protect.

He had never been a hero. Hadn't he tried to warn True of that very fact?

"You are a hero to me." Soft. Husky.

Jake shook his head. *Tell her.* Was that his conscience talking? Yeah, it was. Whispering for him to tell her that he'd taken the case because he wanted her. Because he'd always been a bit obsessed with True Blakely, and he'd seen his chance to finally get close to her when she'd appeared in his office. "I'm not." Ragged. He let go of her wrist and, once more, stood by the bed. The lamp light hit his body.

True sat up. Her gaze drifted over him and lingered on the scars that marked his chest. His stomach.

He had other scars on his back. Not nice and clean lines. In battle, there wasn't time for *clean.* He'd been sewed up as the world exploded around him.

Should he tell her that he'd thought of her during those dark times? That he'd wondered what sweet True Blakely was doing, how she was?

If she was happy?

Her hand reached out and her soft fingers trailed over the scar that cut across his right hip. A bullet graze. That scar wasn't so bad. The bullet had just ripped the skin away as he leapt for cover. Hadn't damaged the muscle or bone.

But her touch had him sucking in a breath even as his entire body tensed.

"You were hurt so many times." Her eyes were on his scars. "I'm sorry."

Why the hell was she sorry?

Before he could ask, she leaned forward. Her lips pressed to the scar on his hip. He looked down at her.

Sweets, you are way too close to another part of my anatomy.

Her hair slid over said part of his anatomy. And when her silken locks teased his dick, a low rumble broke from Jake. At the sound, she looked up at him. Looked up with her body still leaning toward him. With his dick way too close to her mouth.

He didn't say a word. *I should. I'm supposed to say some comforting shit.* He'd never tried to comfort anyone before. But this was different. This was True.

She stared at him. Then, a slow smile curved her lips. A sensual smile.

"True?" Her name came out so rough that it was more a growl than anything else.

She slid from the bed.

Okay, okay. He sucked in a breath. This was—

She went to her knees in front of him. Her fingers curled around his dick. Ever so lightly, as if she was afraid she'd hurt him. Hah. *Not happening.*

"If I need to slow down, say *sleigh bells.*" She leaned forward. Her breath blew lightly over the head of his cock. "And if you want more, say *jingle.*"

Hell, *hell.* True was about to take his dick into her mouth? "True, I—"

She opened her mouth and took his dick inside.

Jingle. Jingle. Jingle!

His hands clamped around her shoulders. She was hesitant, licking and sucking carefully and driving him absolutely insane because *True was going down on him.* His True. His dick pushed deeper into her mouth. She sucked and pulled with her lips and licked with her tongue even as her soft fingers squeezed the base of his cock.

So good. Too good.

True was on her knees before him. Licking him. Sending him hurtling toward release, and he would be coming in her mouth. Exploding soon and he had to—

"True!" Jake pulled back.

She blinked at him. Her lips were swollen. Wet. "Didn't you like it?"

Like it? Like. It? "On the bed." Snarled.

She blinked again. Then scrambled onto the bed.

He yanked open the nightstand drawer. Shoved on a condom in two seconds. Then he stood by the edge of the bed. He caught her legs and pulled her toward him.

"Aren't you..." Her tongue darted out. "Aren't you getting in bed, too?"

No, he was going to fuck her right there.

He pulled her even closer to the edge of the mattress. Spread her wide and stared at her pretty sex. *Mine.*

"What did you say?"

Had he said that part out loud?

His cock shoved against her quivering core. She looked so delicate and sexy, and he watched as she opened for him. As his dick sank inside.

As he took her.

And as she took him.

Slowly. Inch by inch. Her inner muscles resisted a bit, but he strummed her clit. He bent to lick her beautiful breasts. He made her melt for him so that she'd take his dick all the way inside. She had to be sore. He'd worked her so hard during the night.

Because I can't get enough of True. I may never get enough of True.

A gentleman wouldn't fuck her so relentlessly.

True once said it would be disappointing if I was a gentleman. Or something like that. And he certainly didn't want to disappoint her.

Jake was pretty much beyond thought. Just focused on feeling *her*.

He sank balls deep into her. Her breath released on a soft whoosh and her eyes locked on him. He wanted to cut loose and thrust again and again and again until they were both lost to oblivion. But...

But he slowly withdrew. Until only the head of his cock lodged into her.

Then he sank back into her.

One inch at a time.

His fingers stroked her clit. Slow, light strokes.

He withdrew. Ever so slowly.

"Jake!" She thrashed beneath him. "You're playing with me!"

No, never. *I'm keeping you.* He sank back into her. A little faster than before. A little harder.

True's sex clamped so tightly around him that he was sure his sanity might shatter at any second. *Definitely my control. It's gonna shatter. I'm barely holding on.*

"Jingle! Please, *jingle!*" Her hips surged up against him.

He couldn't have True begging. Never that. So he gave her what she wanted. What they both needed. When he drove into her, it was faster. Harder. Her hips lifted off the bed. Her mouth parted on a gasp.

The fingers that had been working her clit stopped being quite so gentle and slow. He gave her the fast, relentless strokes that he knew she craved. Her hips shoved against him. Her sex took him and squeezed as if she'd never let go. Just what he wanted.

The bed groaned. She chanted his name. Her body strained against his.

She took me in her mouth. Now she's taking every inch of me in that tight, hot body.

He watched his dick sink into her. Watched and watched.

She came. Her hips jerked against his, and his name spilled from her in the cry *he* craved. As Jake felt the contractions of her inner muscles around him, he let go. He pounded into her with all the lust that he couldn't contain. The primal need. Over and over, he sank into her until he exploded on a release so intense that the entire world seemed to erupt around him. And as he poured into her, he could not stop the one rumbling word that broke from him.

"Mine."

* * *

SOMETHING WAS RINGING.

True opened her eyes and squinted against the light that poured in from the nearby blinds.

The ringing continued.

Not jingle bells.

Jingle.

Her breath shuddered out as she bolted upright. Upright in a big bed. A bed that she was currently sharing with Jake.

A naked Jake.

And I'm naked, too.

Naked, in the bright light of day.

Jake threw out a hand and grabbed the phone on the nightstand. She vaguely remembered him bringing the phone into the bedroom at some random point in the night.

He put the phone to his ear. "What?" A growl.

A sexy growl. Because he was sexy. Always. But especially first thing in the morning. Her wide eyes swept over him. The stubble on his jaw just made him look hotter. Tougher. The sheet dipped near his waist and exposed all of his wonderful muscles. That ten pack. And his dark eyes were—

Right on me.

"True's place is not a crime scene anymore. Check. Yeah, yeah, we'll go over there. She'll look around. I want her to do a thorough search and make sure nothing was taken. I *know* she scanned the house before, Harris. I was fucking there, remember? But I want a *thorough search.*"

Cold air teased her nipples and had True grabbing for the covers and hauling them over her body.

Jake frowned at her.

She became aware of the aches and pains in her body. In parts of her body that didn't usually ache. *Oh, the things we did last night.* Things that made her blush a fiery red now. True jumped from the bed. She hauled the covers with her. Where were her panties?

In the den. You stripped in the den. Her cheeks burned even more.

His frown turned darker. "Oh, yes. I have my eyes on her."

His eyes were on her. His hands *had* been all over her during the night. And his dick had been *in* her. Not that Harris needed to know any of that information.

How many times did we make love?

Only, it wasn't love. It had been sex. Basic. Primitive. Mind-blowing. Totally worth the aches this morning.

"I'll be keeping her close, you don't need to worry about that. *You* just remember to keep me in the loop with anything you uncover." A pause. Jake's eyes never left her face. "Yeah. Anyone coming after her will need to go through me. Count on it." He hung up the phone.

She continued to stand by the bed, clutching the covers, and curling her toes against the hardwood floor.

Jake tossed the phone back on the nightstand. He quirked one brow. Then he climbed out of the bed—completely naked—and moved to stand in front of her. The man's dick was fully erect. *How* could he be fully erect after what they'd done? Talk about some serious stamina.

"True, True, True...eyes up here."

He caught me staring at his dick. Her eyes whipped up to his face.

He smiled at her. "Don't you look horrified?" The smile didn't reach his eyes. "Having regrets already?"

Her lips parted in surprise.

"Figured it would happen." A nod of his head. "I'm hardly the type for you to—"

"You don't regret the best sex of your life." Her voice was low. Husky. She cleared her throat. "You savor it. You cherish it."

His eyes widened.

She probably shouldn't have said that stuff. At least she'd stopped herself from saying the rest. *And you never, ever forget it.*

Even though the sex had been incredible for her, Jake might have felt differently. *But would he have, uh, gone so many times with me if he hadn't been enjoying himself?*

"If it was the best..." Jake leaned toward her. "Then why the hell do you suddenly look so scared?"

She wasn't scared. Not of Jake. Never of him. But... "I've never had a one-night stand before."

His expression hardened.

"Not exactly sure how this should work. I think I'm probably supposed to be a whole lot more casual and relaxed." But *casual* and *relaxed* didn't cover any of the feelings ricocheting through her.

His hand lifted. Sank into the thickness of her hair as he lowered his head toward her. "That wasn't a one-night stand."

Her heart slammed hard into her chest. "It wasn't?"

"Not even close."

Her heartbeat just raced faster.

"You think once was gonna be enough for me?" Jake rumbled.

"Um, technically, it was a lot more than once."

His eyes gleamed at her. "I went easy on you."

What? If that had been easy, just how did the man describe *hard*?

"Since it had been a while for you and I knew you needed your sleep, I held back."

Held back? He was joking, wasn't he? Only it didn't look like he was.

Jake's lips brushed over hers. "If I'd had my way, my cock would have been in you all night long."

Her sex seemed to clench.

"Are you sore, sweets?"

"A little."

"I'm sorry." Another brush of his lips. He eased away from her. "Want me to promise to keep my hands off you for today?"

"Don't you dare."

He smiled. The grin reached his eyes. Lightened the darkness. "And *that's* why it's not a one-night stand. I want you too much. And you—you still want me, don't you?"

She managed a nod. She also kept clutching the covers to her body.

His grin widened. "You know I've seen every inch of you, right?"

Her hold tightened even more on the covers.

"Kissed every inch, too."

He had. Oh, he had.

"I'll be doing it again," he vowed. "But we are *more* than sex. Understand that. You would never be a one-night stand for me." His tone was suddenly flat. Serious. His grin had vanished.

"What am I?" True wanted to pull the question back as soon as it slipped from her mouth.

His phone rang again.

"Don't you know?" Jake murmured.

She had no clue. Thus, the question.

Another demanding ring.

Her head dipped toward it. "You should get that."

He reached for the phone. He spared a quick glance at the image on the screen before he swiped his finger over the phone's surface and put it to his ear. "Perry, what do you have for me?"

True used that moment to escape. A fast and desperate retreat into the safety of the bathroom.

But his words chased her. That low, rumbling...*Don't you know?*

No, she didn't know what she was to him. She *did* know what he was coming to be to her.

Too much. Everything.

A man I could love.

Not just a boy that she dreamed about. A man who had become something very different and far more important.

And that just absolutely terrified her.

* * *

"The ex-husband isn't in Atlanta," Perry informed him. "I got some of your Atlanta contacts to nose around for us. The guy is on a holiday vacation. Supposed to be at some cabin up in Colorado until the new year."

"I want that confirmed, and by confirmed—I want you talking to someone who has actually seen his ass in Colorado." Jake wanted a visual on the ex.

"On it." Excitement hummed in Perry's voice. "This is a real case. A *murder*. And a kidnapping. Can you believe it?"

He could believe it, all right. "A woman is in danger, Perry. Try not to sound like you just opened the best Christmas present in the world, would you?"

"Sorry." He didn't sound sorry. He still sounded far too excited. "I'm still digging into the financials of the people at the museum. So far, nothing is turning up. But I won't stop digging."

"Good. Don't."

"And I'll report to you as soon as I learn anything else."

Jake's eyes were on the closed bathroom door. She'd run from him. He didn't like that. He liked even less that the woman had thought she was a one-night stand for him. So wrong.

She was his end game.

It was time for her to start realizing that fact.

I need to take True on a freaking date. He'd promised her ice skating. Instead, he'd fucked her all night long. Yeah, okay, fine, maybe he could get where she'd been worried that he was just interested in sex.

As soon as I stop the bastard after her, I will make every single one of True's Christmas dreams come true. Just call him Santa Claus. After all, he did have the suit shoved in his laundry room.

He ended the call. The bathroom door cracked open. True peeked at him.

She was so beautiful with her disheveled hair and bright eyes and her plump lips. He closed in on her, and his gaze dipped to her throat.

A faint, red mark still remained on her skin. A mark he'd made with his mouth.

"What's the plan?" True asked him as she continued to grip the covers to her body.

The plan...

Charm you. Protect you. Convince you to fall hopelessly in love with me.

"Jake?"

He cleared his throat. "We search your house. We go over every attack you've had, and we investigate every person in your life. We find out who the hell is after you, and I rip out his heart."

She blinked those big, blue eyes of hers. "Maybe we should lock him up in jail?"

"Sure, that, too." Lock him up and make certain he never got out again. After Jake ripped out his heart. "You'll be safe while we hunt. I'll protect you."

"I know." Soft. "I trust you, remember?"

I trust you.

Maybe one day soon, she'd be saying...

I love you.

Huh. How about that? Turned out, he *did* want something very badly for Christmas. True's love.

Time to fight dirty for it.

Chapter Ten

"Tis the season...to solve a murder."
– Detective Harris Avery (What? I wanted a quote, too.)

THE COPS HAD LEFT UP A LINE OF YELLOW POLICE TAPE near True's front door. Jake saw it the instant he stepped out of his vehicle. The yellow tape definitely clashed with the festive garland that True had hung up around her entranceway. He'd barely noticed the garland on his last visit to her place. The garland *inside* on her bannisters? Yeah, he'd seen that stuff. But he hadn't paid much attention the house's exterior decorations.

Probably because he'd been too focused on her. And then on the dead body. Dead bodies tended to distract people.

He walked around the vehicle and raised his hand to open True's car door for her.

Someone is in the black BMW. The one parked in front

of her neighbor's house. Only Jake didn't think that driver was a guest of the neighbor.

Jake's hand pulled away from the door. He turned toward the BMW.

The BMW's driver side door opened.

And True opened her door, too. "Jake? What's wrong?"

A man climbed from the BMW. Tall. With carefully styled black hair, wearing a blue sweater and khakis, and aviator sunglasses perched on his nose, he turned his head and seemed to zero in on Jake.

Then the fool began walking toward Jake. A slightly unsteady walk. And maybe those aviators were a little lopsided on his nose.

"What is he doing here?" Horror filled True's voice. "Richard shouldn't be in Rosewood!"

Richard. The ex. No, he shouldn't be in Rosewood. Richard's happy ass should be up in Colorado. He should not be making his way determinedly across the road and straight toward True.

She climbed out of the SUV. Stood at Jake's side. She grabbed for his hand.

Automatically, he looked down. True was holding his hand. His fingers tightened around hers.

"True!" Richard began jogging toward them.

No, toward *her*.

"True! I've been waiting for you!"

Oh, had he?

Richard staggered to a stop right in front of True. And Jake. Richard whipped off his sunglasses and shoved them into the right pocket of his khakis. His bloodshot eyes locked on her. "You didn't come home last night," he accused her.

"No," Jake said, voice flat. "She didn't. Because she was with me."

Richard's glare jumped to him. "Who the fuck are you? And why are you dragging *my wife* home after some all-nighter?"

Oh, no. This SOB did not just say that shit to me.

"I'm not your wife," True fired back. "We're divorced, and you know it, Richard."

Jake stared back at the other man. And smiled. *Richard.* Wasn't the shortened version of that name... "Dick," he said with a nod. "Yeah, *Dick,* she's not your wife. And as for who I am? I'm the—"

"He's my b—" True began.

Maybe she'd been about to say *bounty hunter*. But Jake finished his words before she could, and he very clearly proclaimed, "Boyfriend."

Richard gaped at him.

"I'm the boyfriend," Jake repeated. "The man True was with all night long. Last night. And the night before." His fingers tightened on hers. "Where True goes, I go. Now that we understand who I am and why I'm here...why the fuck are *you* here?"

Rage twisted Richard's face. "Y-you're screwing my wife?"

"I prefer to think of it as making her scream as she comes for me, over and over again."

"Jake!" True snapped.

And Richard *snapped,* too. As in, went crazy right in front of Jake. The prick drew back his fist and came in swinging it.

The problem with the swing? Well, *problems* with it? Problem one was that the guy couldn't swing for shit. Couldn't make a strong fist for shit. Another problem was that Richard's wild and spinning blow might just accidentally hit True.

And that wasn't happening on Jake's watch. He moved quickly to shield True with his body because that fist was flying far too recklessly.

The fast movement protected True and resulted in Richard getting in one lucky punch to Jake's jaw.

"*Jake!*" True cried.

Such a weak-ass punch.

Jake smiled at the ex. "Is it my turn now?"

Richard was winding his arm up like he'd punch again.

"I think I get a turn," Jake decided. "Fair is fair, after all."

But Richard clearly did not agree. His fist flew at Jake once more.

Jake caught it in mid-air. "Haven't you ever heard that you should use your *words* to settle an argument, *prosecutor*? This is just bad form." And Jake squeezed the fist he held. Hard.

Richard paled.

"Bad form because you don't know how to punch." Jake had used his right hand to catch Richard's flying punch. Now Jake pulled back his left, and he drove it hard into Richard's stomach. An *oomph* broke from Richard as he doubled over. "That's how you punch," Jake added with a nod. "And I was using my weak hand because I am a sweetheart like that."

Richard stumbled away from him.

"Should I try with my right hand?" Jake asked politely.

"No!" True jumped in front of him. The woman actually put her body between him and her ex. "Stop this, right now."

All amusement fled because True had just put herself within grabbing distance of her asshole ex. Before that *dick* could put his hands on her, Jake wrapped his fingers around her waist, lifted her up, and put her back behind him. "He doesn't touch you. Never again." Then he faced the jerk once more even as he ordered, "Call Harris, True. Get the cops here, now."

"True, *don't!*" Richard bit out. "I'm here for you! I came back because I need you."

Behind him, Jake heard her calling Harris. Good.

"You need her, huh?" Jake drawled as he cast a disgusted glance over the ex. "How long have you been here in town, needing her?"

"I-I...a few days."

Days? "Long enough to stake out her house? To maybe go inside and kill the bastard you hired to stalk her while you were busy with work in Atlanta?"

"What?" Richard shook his head. He almost fell on his ass, but managed to stay upright at the last moment. "I have no idea what you're talking about. True—*hang up the phone.*" He sidestepped so he could try and see her better.

Jake just moved to the side, too. "Were you at the museum last night?" he asked the ex.

Richard hesitated.

Sonofabitch, he was there.

"I just needed to see True! I knew she'd been working there so I stopped by!"

"And how'd you know that? How'd you know where she worked?"

Richard didn't answer.

"Did you know because you've had Dylan Dunn stalking her?"

Richard flinched.

Like that is not at all suspicious. Like everything about the jerk and his stalking ass wasn't suspicious. The creep had just been parked outside of her house, waiting for her?

"True, I came to the museum, but I didn't see you in the crowd! Just saw kids and a damn Santa. So I came back here to wait on you." Richard's hands fisted at his sides. "Only you never showed up. I was here all night long. *You never showed.*"

The ex needed to check that anger. "Yeah, True didn't show due to the fact that she was with me."

True's fingers pressed to Jake's back. "Uniformed cops are close. Harris said they'd be here soon."

"You seriously think you're going to have *me* arrested? *Me?*" Richard laughed. A high, grating sound. "I'll say he swung first, True. I'll get your boyfriend arrested. I'm a prosecutor, people will believe me. People will—"

Jake shook his head.

"What?" Richard barked.

"Her neighbor has one of those handy doorbell cameras." He'd found out about it from Harris. Unfortunately, nothing had been on the camera the night Dylan Dunn had been killed. *Probably because Dylan and his murderer both came in through the back of True's house.* So the neighbor's doorbell camera hadn't spotted them. But right then, where Richard was standing...a perfect vantage point. "Smile, Dick. You're on camera."

And, damn if the fool didn't try to take yet another swing at Jake. Had the man not heard the words Jake had clearly enunciated? This time when the prick swung, there was no missing the scent of whiskey that clung to Richard.

Jake dodged the blow and because he was tired of bullshit, he drove a hard right cross straight to Richard's jaw. The dick went down, groaning, and he didn't get up.

Jake crouched next to his prey. "The cops are coming, and before they arrive, you're going to understand some very, very important facts."

Richard blinked blearily at him.

"She's not your wife any longer. She's not your anything. You don't stalk her. You don't scare her. You don't get *near* her again."

"True!" Richard shrieked.

Jake didn't even like the prick saying her name. "You're the dumbass who lost her," Jake rasped. "And I'm the lucky bastard who has her now." He never took his gaze from Richard's face. "I'm also the bastard who knows how to fight in order to keep her. I went easy on you today." For the camera. Because he knew how to wait and how to drive a man to attack. *Thanks for the footage. Your ass will be in a cell soon.* "I'll never go easy again." *You've been warned.*

Jake would offer no additional warnings.

He rose and shook his head in disgust as he studied the sprawled ex. "Really, True? What the hell did you see in this guy?" Jake turned to face her.

Horror filled her expression as she stared down at her ex.

"I'm sorry, True!" Richard cried out. And, yep, some of those words slurred. The more he spoke, the more slurred his voice became. "S-sorry for the affair! Sorry for hurting you! *I'm s-sorry about the baby!*"

Jake stiffened. Every muscle went rock hard.

What baby?

"I want you back. N-nothing is the same without you. I want you back! Please, True. Please. Give me another chance!"

True shook her head. "That's not ever going to happen."

In the distance, a siren wailed.

And Jake realized that wasn't just horror on True's face. It was pain. Grief.

What baby?

Jake stepped toward True. Lifted his hand and carefully curled his fingers under her chin. "True? You okay?"

Her lower lip trembled. Jake pulled her against him. Held her tight. Curled his body around hers and hugged her. He could feel her pain, and he didn't know how to take it away.

He was still holding her when the cops arrived.

* * *

THERE WERE some hurts that never ended. Sure, they'd dull with time. The sharpness couldn't cut like a knife forever. But the ache would remain.

Richard's appearance...and his words...they'd stirred up the past.

I'm s-sorry about the baby.

She stood on her porch and watched her ex-husband get loaded into the back of a patrol car. Talk about how the mighty had fallen. Richard had always been the man who prosecuted criminals. But he'd just been cuffed. And he'd be heading to the station soon.

She'd fallen for him so long ago because she'd believed Richard when he said that he wanted to make the world a better, safer place. But somewhere along the way, he'd stopped being the idealistic guy with the big dreams. His ambition had gotten the better of him. The cases he'd taken had been less about serving justice. More about getting his name splashed in the media.

"Guy wouldn't submit to a breathalyzer. Shouting about how he's a lawyer and knows his rights." Harris stood on her sidewalk and glanced up at True. "But we found two empty whiskey bottles in his car. He reeks of the stuff. We also got the footage from the neighbor's camera." A wave of his hand toward the brick house to the right. "We can arrest him for assault. Dude is most definitely drunk and disorderly."

Jake stood near Harris. When True glanced at him, though, she found Jake's eyes locked on her. No emotion covered his face. "You want him arrested, True?"

She wrapped her arms around her body. "He was at the museum last night."

Jake nodded. "We both heard him admit that."

"Do you think he put me in the sarcophagus?" Would Richard do something like that? Once, she would have said no, absolutely not. But then again, she would have also said that he'd never try to assault someone, yet he'd gone at Jake right in front of her.

And Jake had so easily taken Richard down.

"I'm gonna grill him like hell when I get him to the station," Harris vowed. "I can also guarantee that he'll be in holding and interrogation for as long as possible. His drunk ass isn't going to be getting out of the station anytime soon."

Her breath expelled in a rush. "Thanks for coming here so quickly, Harris."

Harris's gaze cut to the patrol car as it pulled away. "You know your ex looks suspicious as hell," Harris told her.

Yes, she knew that.

"He ever pull shit like this with you before?" Harris pushed as his attention shifted back to her. "Did he ever get rough with you?"

A growl broke from Jake.

"No." A negative shake of her head. "He's never been physically violent with me." Her lips pressed together. "I would have left him if he had been."

"You *did* leave him," Harris pointed out. "There more to that story?"

There was more, but nothing relevant to Harris. "He never physically hurt me."

"You can't say that for sure." Harris rubbed his index finger along the bridge of his nose. "If it turns out that he's the perp who locked you in that old coffin, I'd say he was all about some physical cruelty."

Richard wouldn't do that.

Would he?

Harris ambled away. Her neighbors had all finally gone back inside their homes, too. They'd come out when the cops arrived. Everyone liked a good show.

Everyone but her.

True's shoulders sagged as she turned and made her way inside. The yellow tape was still up, and she yanked it down before she crossed the threshold. Her house was still. Too quiet. And a faint odor lingered in the air.

From the dead body?

The door closed softly behind her. She waited, knowing what question would come. Almost hating it.

"What baby?" Jake asked her softly.

Her shoulders stiffened as pain from her past washed over her. "I was going to call him Lucas." It hurt so much to say his name. "I lost him right at thirteen weeks. And nothing has ever hurt me more." Not even when she'd lost her mother. Then her father.

Losing Lucas...seeing the blood slide from her and knowing there was nothing she could do to stop it...nothing she could do to save her baby...

Jake's hands curled around her shoulders. "I am so sorry," he told her.

She nodded. Her eyes closed, the better to hold in the tears. "I went to the hospital by myself. Richard was working on a case." There had always been some big case with him. "Afterwards, he acted...like it was nothing. Like everything could carry on. He wouldn't talk about the baby at all. We'd tried for a year to get pregnant. I wanted that baby so much, and I was grieving but he wasn't. And that was when I realized..." She stopped. "Sometimes, people don't have the same dreams." Her eyes opened, and she turned in his arms. "I want to be Santa Claus."

He frowned at her. "Sweets, I am not sure I am following."

"I want to put up a tree and have presents wrapped and waiting for my child on Christmas morning. I want to hear laughter and see wonder in a kid's eyes. I want to go trick-or-treating with him. With her. I want to cheer at a football game or clap at a dance recital. Or cry at a theater show. I want kids. Richard...he didn't. Today—today is the first time that he has ever said he was sorry I lost the baby. It's the first time that he's ever told me he was sorry for anything."

A muscle flexed along Jake's clenched jaw. "I should have kicked his ass so much more."

A half laugh, half sob escaped her. "He's not worth it." Not worth getting bruised knuckles.

"You love him?"

She shook her head. "A very long time ago, a different me fell in love with a different him. We are not the same people any longer. Or, hell, maybe I never knew him." Not who he really was. Maybe he'd just been pretending? And maybe she'd just been looking for someone *to* love. "My parents died. I had no other family. I was lost. And Richard said he needed me." But she'd grown up over the years. She'd learned important lessons.

Need wasn't love.

Ambition wasn't love.

She'd tried to make their marriage work. But when your husband was making out with his legal secretary...

Screw him.

That had been the last straw. She'd left and hadn't looked back. "I'm not crying for him." The tears had slipped out even though she'd tried to stop them. "I'm crying for me. Because I wasted too much time. Because *I* wanted Lucas." Because she always would want him. "I'm crying for my baby and for everything that could have been."

His fingers caught her tears. Wiped them carefully away. "I will give you a baby."

Again, that half laugh, half sob came from her. He wasn't serious. "What?"

His gaze never wavered. "I would give you anything in the world you wanted. When will you realize that?"

She couldn't breathe. He seemed so serious. But he wasn't. Was he? "Jake?"

"That dick out there didn't deserve you. He hurt you, and, sweets, I will gladly hurt *him* for you. And if it turns out that he is the one who tied you up at the museum, if he committed murder right here in your house..."

Her gaze automatically jerked toward her tree. Only, no tree was there. It had been removed. Probably because of all the blood on it?

"Harris took it away," Jake explained as he followed her gaze. "They had to saw off branches for evidence. He said—hell, it was a wreck by the time they were done. I'll get you another tree, True. A bigger one."

"I don't need a tree." She needed for the fear to end in her life. She needed to feel safe. She needed...

Jake.

Her lips pressed together. After a moment, she released a low breath and said, "I'm supposed to go and search through my stuff upstairs." That had been the plan, right? To double-check everything. Make sure nothing was missing. Before, nothing had *seemed* disturbed. She'd even checked her jewelry before the place had been turned into crime scene central. "I'll, um, go do that." She pulled away from Jake and turned for the stairs. Then she hesitated. "Is it okay if I stay at your condo again tonight?" True peeked over her shoulder at him. "I don't exactly relish the thought of coming back to the place where a man was murdered."

"You can stay with me for as long as you want."

Relief rolled through her. "Thank you." She grabbed for the banister and hurried up a few of the steps.

"True."

Her hold on the banister tightened. She stilled on the fifth step and partially turned to look back at him. Jake had moved to the bottom of the staircase.

"He was a fool to hurt you."

She swallowed.

"*Any* man who hurts you is a fool. A smart bastard would count himself lucky for every second he spent with you. He'd go out of his way to make you happy. Because your smile is one of the best fucking things in this world."

Surprise had her eyes widening. "That's probably the nicest thing anyone has ever said to me."

"I don't do nice very well. I tend to screw it up when I try." He squared his shoulders. "I'll never be the *nice* guy. I'm not him. But I am the guy who will do whatever it takes to protect you. You can count on me, always. Know that."

"Thank you, Jake." She smiled at him. Then she hurried up the stairs.

* * *

Jake watched True until she disappeared at the top of the stairs. Her smile lingered in his mind. He raked a hand through his hair. "Best fucking thing in the world."

She was the best thing in his world. And no one was going to hurt her.

Not some dick ex.

Not some mystery stalker.

No one.

He turned and glared at the spot where her Christmas tree had been. True liked Christmas. But this year, every bit of magic was being drained from her holiday. Dammit, she'd been *crying*. Breaking the heart that he'd forgotten about.

His hand pressed to his chest—where Jake could have sworn he felt an ache. Or maybe a thawing.

Hell, is this how the Grinch had felt?

Because being with True made him think that just maybe...his freaking heart was growing.

Growing. Thawing. Melting.

For her.

Son of a nutcracker. He was going to have to save Christmas for True. Some days, a bounty hunter's work was just never, ever done.

Chapter Eleven

"Who cares about the nice list? Being naughty is way more fun. True story."
– Jake Hale (Ahem, True story...see what I did there?)

"Perry, Perry, slow down and listen to me, would you?" Jake snapped into his phone as he made his way to the back door of True's house.

"I can't find him," Perry informed him, voice miserable. "I can't actually get anyone near Richard's cabin to confirm that they've seen him. I am not giving up, boss, I will continue until I have proof—"

"Yeah, give up." Jake frowned when he saw the back door. The *open* back door. Had the cops really left her house unsecured that way? Jake reached out a hand and pulled the door toward him.

The lock had been smashed to hell and back.

That explains how the killer got inside. Jake would make immediate arrangements for a new lock to be installed.

"Did you just ask me to give up?" Perry's voice broke. "Are you—are you firing me, sir?"

"No." Jeez. The kid was such a worrier. "But you aren't going to get proof that Richard Wells is in Colorado because he's not there. The jerk is right here in Rosewood. Just got his ass dragged down to the police station because he was being a drunk and disorderly fool." He studied the shattered lock. A professional would have left minimal signs of intrusion. But her door looked as if someone had just shattered the lock. Burst inside. With no care about leaving evidence or destruction behind.

You wanted in awful badly, didn't you?

"He's there?" Perry's voice cracked.

"Yeah. So stop trying to locate him. Harris is gonna grill him at the station." Time to shift Perry's focus. "Got a new job for you."

"Uh, I'm still running financials on everyone at the museum. Not seeing any red flags, but sometimes you just have to dig really deep."

"Yeah, yeah. Dig deep. Keep doing that. But, also, I need a Christmas tree."

Silence.

"You heard me, didn't you, Perry?" Jake peered beyond True's back patio. Thick trees surrounded the rear of her property. It would be too easy for someone to hide in those trees.

"I-I *think* I heard you. You said you wanted a-a Christmas tree."

"A really big one." It would need to be bigger than the one True had lost. "Maybe twelve feet? Fourteen? And can you get it delivered to my place? As soon as possible?" Was that too much to ask? Maybe. Probably. Whatever.

"Who is this?" Perry suddenly demanded in a rush. "And what have you done with my boss?"

"Cut the humor, smart-ass."

"Yes, sir, Mr. Scrooge, sir."

Hadn't he told the kid to cut the humor? Jake tightened his grip on the phone. "I don't want some sad-ass tree like the one in our office."

"That is a beautiful tree!"

Great. Now Perry seemed offended.

"And I had practically no budget." Perry sniffed. "Considering what I had to work with, the tree in our office is a miracle. Ahem, speaking of miracles, you can't really expect me to find a twelve-foot Christmas tree—"

"A live one. I want it to smell like Christmas."

Again, silence. Then, "Sir, are you feeling well? Have you, by chance, recently hit your head?"

His head was just fine. "Money isn't an issue. Go big or go ho-ho-home, am I right?"

"You just made a Christmas joke."

Yeah, shit, he had. "Use the company credit card. Deliver the tree to my place, ASAP. You get it decorated, and there is a Christmas bonus in it for you."

"I do not know what is happening right now, but I am both excited and scared," Perry informed him. "Though that is often the way I feel when I work at our agency. Especially when you tell me that you're tracking a murderer."

I'm tracking a murderer right now. I'm just taking a small Christmas detour for True because her tears and her pain make me want to break something.

Footsteps rushed behind him. "Jake!" True's breathless voice called.

"Got to go," Jake told Perry. "Get the tree." Low. Gruff.

He hung up the phone and spun just as True came rushing right up to him.

Her eyes were wide, her lips parted, and her breath heaved a little too fast from what looked like a run she'd taken in order to reach him.

"I was wrong." True grabbed his arms. "I didn't think anything had been taken, but I just checked through my briefcase. It was upstairs. And—*I was wrong.*"

Now they were getting somewhere. "Okay, sweets, don't leave me in suspense. What was taken?"

"I'd brought home some inventory lists from the museum. I'd intended to go over the lists during the holiday break so I could see exactly what items I had to work with as I made plans for reenergizing the place." A shake of her head sent her hair sliding over her shoulders. "But some of the papers are missing. All of the inventory lists aren't there."

The killer had taken inventory lists from the museum?

True was attacked twice in the museum.

Dots were connecting in Jake's mind and forming a picture he didn't like. "These inventory lists—are you the only person who has recently taken a look at what is and what is not stored in the backrooms of the museum?"

"Well, yes." Her gaze searched his. "It's my job. Like I said, I want to reenergize things there. Part of doing that means pulling items out of storage and putting them on display. Giving new life to things that have been forgotten."

Suspicions swirled in his mind. "You can't give new life to something that isn't there." Maybe they'd been looking at this all wrong. Maybe it wasn't about True—about some obsession that a person had gotten with her. For her.

Maybe...maybe it was about stopping True. Before she uncovered a crime.

Then why did Dylan Dunn wind up as the dead one?

"We need to get back in that museum," True murmured.

Damn straight, they did. "Tell me that your beautiful, organized heart has copies of the lists that were missing."

"My organized heart has copies of the lists that are missing."

He hauled her close and kissed her. A fast, hard kiss. "Of course, you do."

"Those were the originals in my briefcase." Her eyes gleamed at him. "But I scanned them onto my computer at work because I wanted backups. Some of the notations were so old—I scanned them so I could have them in an updated system. I'm trying to update everything at the museum."

And someone did not like what she was doing. *Because that someone thinks True will discover something she shouldn't.* "Did you tell anyone that you were creating the backups?"

"Aliyah knows."

Aliyah's image flashed through his mind. The wistful smile on her lips as she gazed after her sister and her niece. His gut said the woman was legitimately kind. But with True's life in danger, he needed more than gut instinct.

"I don't think anyone else knows," True added, but there was uncertainty in her voice. Her hands fell away from him. "And before you get all suspicious, whatever is happening, Aliyah isn't involved."

"Are you saying that because she's your friend or because you have some kind of proof?"

"Being my friend is the proof."

He shook his head. "No, sweets, it isn't. People you trust can be the ones to wreck you the hardest."

"It's *not* her." True was adamant. "A *man* shoved me in the sarcophagus. Someone very strong. That wasn't Aliyah."

"Someone wanted your list to vanish. Let's go find out why." He wasn't going to rule out any suspects. Not yet. Maybe more than one person was involved. Everyone would be staying on his damn list.

Including the drunk-ass ex-husband.

Because Richard's sudden appearance was too coincidental. Jake had never believed in coincidences. Not coincidences. Not fate. Not Christmas magic.

Or at least...

Not until the Ghost of Christmas Past walked in my door. Then he'd started to believe in all kinds of new things.

"Before we leave, we're fixing your back door." No way would Jake just rush out and leave it open so someone else could get inside. Thanks, but no thanks. "Then we'll hit the museum."

* * *

"True?" Robert Moss had just unlocked the museum's front door for her. "You're not supposed to be here. The place is closed on Sundays and Mondays, you know that."

And since it was nearing Sunday night...

Surprise, surprise, Robert is on duty again.

Robert stood in the doorway. Though he had unlocked the door, he did not move back so that True and Jake could enter. True forced a smile as she stared at the guard. Robert had always been friendly. Been kind to her. But now she couldn't help but feel suspicious as she gazed at him.

During the car ride to the museum, she and Jake had talked about their possible suspects. *If* this nightmare really was about the museum—and artifacts in the museum—then

Jake believed someone employed at the museum had to be directly involved.

Someone who worked at the museum would've had the access needed to be in the Egyptian display room during the first attack—and the one last night.

But the people who worked there were her friends. There was no way Aliyah was involved. True just would not buy that Aliyah would hurt her. And Robert showed her pictures of his grandchildren all the time. He wasn't some killer.

Was he?

"The cops have the Egyptian room taped off," Robert informed her. "Uniforms just left a bit ago. They told me no one was to go inside that space."

"I'm not going in there," she assured him. That room was the last place she wanted to be. "Just forgot something in my office. Jake and I swung by real fast to pick it up."

Robert frowned.

She held her breath. Lying had never come easily to her. Could Robert tell she was making up the story?

But he nodded. Backed up. "I'm always forgetting stuff, too," Robert told her with a grimace. "Happens to us all."

Her breath rushed out as she hurried inside the museum. As soon as True crossed over the threshold, goosebumps rose on her skin. The place just felt *cold.*

Or maybe being back inside made her feel too scared. She hated that fear because she'd loved working at the museum. Or, she *had* loved it, right up until the moment she'd been locked in a sarcophagus. *Do not think about that right now. Do. Not.*

Jake followed her inside, and he immediately took her hand as they headed for her office.

Robert scrambled and stepped into their path. "You two an item now?"

"I—" True stopped.

"Yes," Jake said. "Some things are damn important in this world. I realized that last night when True vanished." Jake's voice hardened as he added, "Made me understand the full meaning of rage. When I find the creep who put her in that coffin, I am going to make him pay."

Robert swallowed. "I used to be a cop."

"You don't say?" Jake's bland voice.

Robert nodded. "Over in Atlanta. Saw things that made me sick. People can be evil. They'll lie and pretend, and you never know what you're dealing with until it's too late." His hands went to his hips. The keys bounced. "But it's not our job to make others pay. Courts decide who is guilty and innocent."

"He came after True." Flat. "He's guilty, and he'll pay."

Robert's eyes widened as he stepped to the side. "That's some dangerous talk."

"I'm a dangerous man." His hold tightened on True. "Come on, sweets. Let's go pick up the item you forgot."

She hurried away with him but had to glance back over her shoulder. She found Robert's gaze on them. Whispering, she asked Jake, "He wasn't threatening us, was he?" Robert's words replayed in her mind. *People can be evil. They'll lie and pretend, and you never know what you're dealing with until it's too late.*

"Hard to say."

They paused in front of her office. "You *were* threatening him, though, weren't you?" True asked.

He shrugged. "I was making sure my intent was clear." He leaned closer. "You won't be hurt again."

She wanted to push up onto her toes. To kiss him. But...

Not here.

They had a job to do. Jumping Jake's bones was not the job. Finding out who'd been terrorizing her *was* the plan. Turning away from Jake, she fumbled with the lock. After a nervous moment, True managed to open the door and step inside. Automatically, she flipped on the lights when she entered her office, and True hurried toward her desk. She yanked back her chair and she—

Crunch.

True looked down. She'd just stepped on a shattered piece of plastic. There were lots of shattered chunks of plastic and metal on her floor. And wires. Brackets.

"Hell." Jake's hands closed over her shoulders as he carefully pulled her back. "Someone beat us to the backup."

Because her computer had been smashed to pieces in her office.

A knock sounded at her door. Her open door.

Her head whipped up. Robert stood there, frowning. "Did you find what you needed?"

Not even close. "My computer is broken." The files she'd needed had been on the computer. Not saved to some cloud. *On* the hard drive.

Robert edged closer. "How'd that happen?"

Her stomach twisted. *Someone came in and smashed it to pieces.* Someone with access to the museum.

The keys jingled at his waist.

"No worries," Jake said, sounding not even a little bit put out. "I know a guy who can fix this."

He did?

Her head swung back to him.

"My guy is a tech genius," he assured her. "When it comes to computers, there is nothing that he can't recover. He'll get all your files for you." His gaze flickered to Robert.

"No problem at all." A brief pause then, "Let's box it up. He'll have it working for you by Christmas."

* * *

Jake shut the SUV's passenger side door. As he walked around the vehicle, he saluted a watching Robert and whistled as he made his way to the driver's side. He climbed in. Cranked the vehicle.

And was actually prepared when the Christmas music blared at him this time. *Jingle Bell Rock.*

"My computer is in a thousand pieces," True said.

Yep, he was aware. He'd helped pick up those thousand pieces and put them in a box.

"I get that you think your tech buddy is good, but it would take a miracle to fix this."

He reversed the vehicle. Robert was still watching. "Oh, sweets, there is no fixing your computer."

"Uh, then why did we box it up? And shouldn't we have called the cops to report the damage?"

"I'll inform Harris." At the top of his to-do list. He'd make that call in moments. "Not like there are gonna be any prints, though. There haven't been prints left behind at any of the attacks."

"Robert was wearing gloves." Soft.

"You noticed that, too, huh? Gloves, while on duty inside the museum. Fun fashion choice." His grip tightened around the steering wheel. "I know that the computer can't be repaired. You know it can't be repaired. But our friend Robert? If he's the perp we're after, then he now needs to worry that we're going to uncover the truth. That means he may panic. In my experience, panic always leads to mistakes." He'd be informing Harris of exactly what had gone down in the museum. Either Harris would haul Robert in for questioning or the detective would put a tail on the guard.

We need a tail on him. If Harris doesn't do it, then I'll get Perry to track Robert.

"If this is about the museum, about someone stealing from the museum, then why is Richard in town?" True wondered. "I don't get it."

His grip could not get tighter on the wheel. "Maybe that bastard just wants you back. I've heard holidays make people nostalgic as hell. They start thinking about what they've lost. What they don't have. What they want." He waited a beat. "You want that old life of yours back?" Was he holding his breath? Yes, he was.

"I want to go forward. Not back. Richard is not the man I want."

Who do you want? Come on, sweets, say it. Say...

My name.

"He isn't you," she finished softly.

Fuck. "That is the nicest thing anyone has ever said to me." He gave her the same words she'd given to him not too long ago.

"That wasn't nice. It was the truth. If you want to hear something *nice*...then how about this? You're the kindest, bravest man I've ever met. You stood up for me when no one else did, and I won't ever forget that."

What could have been guilt twisted inside of him. *I took the case because I wanted you. Not because I was kind.* He braked at the light and turned his head. He needed to tell her the truth.

But when he looked in her eyes and saw the way that she stared back at him...

People in school used to think I was trash.

She wasn't looking at him like he was trash.

"You're the man I want," True said again.

No, he was not some *nice* sonofabitch. Because a nice guy would not haul her close and kiss her as if his very life depended on the act.

But he did haul her close. He did kiss her with wild need, ferocious hunger, and a desire that could not be quenched.

Screw nice.

He'd stay on the naughty list.

Permanently.

Chapter Twelve

"Be merry, bright, and make love to a hot bounty hunter tonight. I get that isn't a real saying, but...maybe it should be?"
– True Blakely (who intends to make love to a certain hot bounty hunter at the first opportunity)

Perry shot to attention when he saw them approaching the condo. He bounded forward, waving his hands. "Boss, I didn't get to finish! I have the tree inside, but no decorations yet! You aren't supposed to be here so soon! You texted and said you were going to the museum and that I'd have more time."

Yeah, and he'd also just texted to say he was five minutes away. Thus, the reason Perry was outside of the condo, waiting for them. As to the rest of what his assistant had just revealed...Jake let out a long-suffering sigh. "It was a surprise, Perry."

"You coming back early was a surprise? Then why'd you text me?"

Patience. Have patience. "The Christmas tree. It was a surprise."

"But...you asked for it." A furrow appeared between Perry's brows. "How could it be a surprise?"

Jake stepped to the side but kept his grip on the large box—and the broken computer inside the box. When he sidestepped, True waved at his assistant.

"Hi, ma'am," Perry greeted her.

"The surprise was for her," Jake explained.

"Oh."

"Right. Oh."

Perry winced. "Didn't think it made sense that you'd want a tree. You hate Christmas."

True lightly touched Jake's arm. Cold air swirled around them. He swore he could smell the faintest hint of snow. They were due for another downpour. She inched closer.

Snow and strawberries.

"Jake, you got a tree?" True appeared stunned. "For me?"

"Uh, ma'am, technically, I got the tree," Perry informed her. "But it doesn't have decorations. There are a few boxes of lights inside that I left near the tree, but I didn't have time for anything else." He took a quick hop forward. "I was running more background checks on the museum staff. Wanted to let you know that no one is living beyond their means. No one seems to have hit the lottery with a new bank deposit. The financials are all coming back clean." He poked at the box Jake held. "Why are you carrying a broken computer?"

"Because something very important is on the computer."

Perry's mouth kicked up in a half-smile. "You mean something very important *was* on the computer."

Yeah, that was what he meant.

Perry didn't just poke at the box. He started poking around *inside* the box. "The exterior doesn't matter. All this plastic? Big metal chunks? Dump them." More poking. "It's the hard drive that matters most." He tugged something out. "Ugh. Poor baby was beat to hell and back." He pulled the box from Jake's arms. "But I'll see what I can do."

"Hold up." Jake squinted at the kid. "You think you can actually retrieve data?" He'd been bullshitting with Robert. Just trying to make the guy slip up.

"We'll see. Maybe I'll give you a Christmas miracle. Those happen, you know." Perry bobbed his head toward True. "Ma'am. You stay safe tonight." He began to walk back down the small sidewalk.

Jake grabbed his arm.

Perry's eyes widened. "Something wrong?"

Yeah. Me. "I'm an asshole boss."

"No, you're not." An adamant denial. "You're the best boss I've ever had."

"I'm the *only* boss you ever had." And he was too tough on the kid. Dammit.

But Perry shook his head. "I've worked at diners. Car washes. Factories. Been employed by people who didn't give a damn about me." His chin lifted. "Nobody gave a damn, not until you."

Oh, hell, the kid had better not bring up the time he'd—

"You stopped my stepdad from beating the hell out of me."

True sucked in a sharp breath.

"You think I'll ever forget that?" Perry gave a slow shake of his head. "His fist was coming at me, again and again, and I was a scared sixteen-year-old who just wanted to keep my mom safe. Every part of me hurt, and I was curled in a ball because I couldn't stop him." His cheeks darkened. "Then you were there."

Perry had better not cry. That had been one of the rules when Jake hired him. "I was chasing a bounty. That jerk had jumped bail. I was just doing my job."

"You're such a liar sometimes, boss." Perry rolled back his shoulders. His hold on the box never wavered. "You weren't even a full-time bounty hunter back then. You were on leave from your special ops work. You were in Rosewood and doing a favor for the agency's old owner, Lorenzo Lake."

Yeah, he had been doing a favor for a friend. Lorenzo had been overextended, so Jake had stepped in. Who would have known that he'd one day take over the business? Take it over, make the thing thrive. Now, Jake chased bounties for half the state.

"I always kind of thought it was fate that you happened to be working that particular bounty. Saw you as my guardian angel." Perry swallowed. "You pulled my stepdad off me. You knocked him out and had cuffs on him in an instant. You got me to a hospital. You got me *and* my mom a new place to live. You paid the rent for two years while she got her LPN license and while I finished high school. And then you paid for my college."

Jake could feel True's gaze on him. But he didn't look at her. He kept his focus on Perry. The kid who'd wormed his way past his guard, despite Jake's best efforts. "You should have gone to work for one of those tech headhunters who came after you." How many times had he told the kid that very thing?

"Not gonna happen, boss. I'm where I belong." Perry lifted the box higher. "I'll get the information back for you. You'll see. You'll be proud of me."

Fuck. "I already am," Jake groused. Shit, did the kid think he wasn't?

Perry blinked. A lot of blinks.

"Rule number two, Perry," Jake fired at him.

"No tears, yes, sir, but since we violated rule number one, I thought it was okay. Thought we were breaking rules left and right now."

True sidled closer. "You love to break rules, Jake."

Yeah, he did. Sue him. "Don't pick up my bad habits," he warned Perry. "Be better than me."

"No." Perry stared straight at him. "I want to be just like you, sir."

Why the hell would he want to do that?

But Perry gave another nod before he marched away. Jake stared after him, shaking his head.

"What's rule number one?" True asked, voice soft.

"No Christmas trees." But he'd broken that rule when he let Perry bring in their Charlie Brown tree.

And then he'd broken it again today when he asked for a tree to give True.

Yeah, right. Fine. I love to break rules.

"He loves you," True said.

His head swung toward her. Jake gaped at her. He must have misunderstood. Must. Have.

"He does. You can see it on his face. Hear it in his voice. Perry idolizes you."

Jake spun and strode for the condo. "He needs a new idol."

"I don't think he does." She followed him.

Jake stopped in front of the front door. Then, slowly, he turned toward True.

"You're not as bad as you want the world to think." Her hand rose and pressed over his heart. "First, you take my case when no one else will believe me, then you're Santa for the kids, and now, I find out that you're Perry's protector."

He hated remembering that long-ago scene with Perry. "The stepdad was wanted for two robberies and an assault. He was an abusing bastard. He'd broken Perry's arm. Broken two of the kid's ribs. Like I was just going to let him get away with that?"

"No. Not you."

"He wanted Perry to suffer. So I made him suffer instead. The guy knows to never, ever come close to Perry or his mom again."

She searched his gaze. "You're not a bounty hunter because you like chasing down prey."

Don't be too sure. I live for the adrenaline rush. I enjoy the hunt. I'm good at hunting. I'm—

"You do it to make sure the bad guys don't get away. You're a protector at your core." Her hand was still over his heart. "You're Perry's hero, and you're mine, too." She pushed onto her toes.

He bent toward her.

His mouth skimmed over hers. Just a tease. A light taste.

"Thank you, Jake," she murmured.

He didn't want her gratitude.

He unlocked the door. Perry had a key of his own—he'd given it to the guy long ago. Jake shoved open the door and waved for True to enter first. She did, hurrying inside, only to draw up short with a gasp.

Jake followed her and froze, too. He got why she'd gasped. The top of the Christmas tree scraped his ceiling.

"That is the biggest Christmas tree I've ever seen in my life," True declared as her eyes widened.

He could smell the scent of the Christmas tree filling the room.

"How did he even get it inside?" she wondered.

Yeah, that would be an excellent question. Jake had no clue.

She slowly walked closer to the tree. One hand extended as she touched a branch. "You asked him to get a tree, for me?"

Well, it sure as shit hadn't been because Jake wanted it for himself. "You love Christmas."

She slanted a glance back at him. "But you don't."

Jake rolled his shoulders as if the tree didn't matter. *What matters is making True happy.* "Maybe Christmas is growing on me. You lost your tree, so I asked Perry to bring in another one. Simple. No big deal."

"You...wanted to surprise me."

He looked at the giant tree. The slightly lop-sided, giant tree. "Perry has a real good heart on him." Jake cleared his throat. "He's like you. You have a good heart, too."

"So do you."

He'd almost forgotten he had a heart, until his Ghost of Christmas Past had slipped into his office. Now he seemed to feel far too much. With her. Because of her. "We can decorate the tree." A box of lights sat to the side, as promised by Perry. "We'll go buy ornaments and anything else you think we need."

"I think I have what I need."

His gaze flew to her face. She was staring right at him.

Sweets, do not look at me that way. You do, and I'll have

you naked in five seconds. Then I'll be inside you in the next breath.

He backed up a step.

Her brows rose in confusion. "Jake?"

"We put the bait in our trap at the museum. If Robert is guilty, if he's the one who smashed the computer and who trapped you in that sarcophagus, he will come after the computer because he'll want to stop us before we can recover anything. He will be coming here." Robert's possible trip to Jake's place was the reason why—when he'd been talking to Harris on the ride over—the detective had agreed to have undercover units patrol the area. "We need to catch him in the act." Jake took another step back. Green needles were scattered on the hardwood floor and on the rug in front of the fireplace.

I had True on that rug last night. She screamed for me.

"There's something I need to give you," he said. Jake motioned for her to come closer.

She darted closer. She wore black tennis shoes. Faded jeans. An oversized red sweater. Her hair tumbled over her shoulders, and her bright eyes were locked on him. "Give me?" she seemed confused. "I think you just *gave* me a Christmas tree. You don't need to give me anything else."

"This isn't exactly a gift." This was about something that had been bothering him since last night.

If Jake had his way, then, hell, yes, he would gladly stand between True and any threat. Every threat. That was the plan. To be there. To protect her.

But what if I'm not there? As he hadn't been there when she'd been bound and gagged in the Egyptian display room.

"What is it?" She stood right in front of him. Her head tilted to the right.

"You said your attacker was too fast. Too strong for you to get away."

The delicate column of her throat moved. A flash of fear came and went in her eyes. "Yes."

"You ever had a self-defense class, True?"

"No. I-I wanted to sign up for one at the gym once, but life got so busy and I..." Her voice trailed away. "No," she said again. "No, I haven't."

He nodded. "I'm gonna teach you some quick and dirty tips. Then, for Christmas, I'm signing you up for some classes that I want you to take." His gaze remained locked on her. "I don't want you to ever feel helpless again. I want you to be able to fight back. I want you to do as much damage to any bastard who comes at you as you possibly can."

"Who will teach the classes?"

"Me, sweets. I teach self-defense classes at the local community center. I'll be your teacher. The *full* course is what you'll take. But for now, like I said, you'll get my quick and dirty version."

She nodded. "Quick and dirty. All right."

"Show me how he grabbed you."

True blinked. She didn't show him. The fear flickered in her eyes again.

He kept his body loose with an effort. "Are you afraid of me?"

"No."

"Good." His voice was mild. Careful. *Because it's True.* "You don't ever need to be afraid of me. I'd sooner gnaw off my own arm than ever so much as bruise you. I'll show you some techniques, but if you get uncomfortable and you need a break...well, you remember what to say, don't you?"

The safe words she'd picked out before. Right in this same room.

Fear didn't flare in her eyes. A flash of heat—of lust—did. "Sleigh bells."

"That's right. You know I'll stop instantly."

She nodded. Some of the tension slid from her delicate shoulders.

"Show me how he caught you," Jake urged her.

True turned away. "I was running. He came up behind me."

Jake edged closer behind her.

"H-he put a hand on my mouth. He did it so fast that I couldn't scream."

Jake covered her mouth with his hand.

Immediately, she stiffened.

He lifted his fingers, hovering them about an inch in front of her mouth. "Where was his other hand?"

"He curled his arm around my stomach and jerked me back."

Jake curled his arm around her stomach. He pulled her back against him. Her body trembled. "Don't be afraid of me," he rasped. "You said you trusted me, remember?"

She nodded.

"Good." He pressed a kiss to the back of her head. "I want you to understand that it doesn't matter how much bigger your opponent is. Everyone has a weak spot."

"Even you?" Her soft question.

"Hell, yes." *You are my weak spot.* "If someone is covering your mouth and you want that creep's hand gone, you reach for the weak spot." Carefully, he put his hand over her mouth. "The pinky, sweets. Do you know how easily a pinky breaks? You grab it, and you wrench it as hard as you can. When you yank that pinky and it breaks, that might be enough to distract the bastard so you can get away. His weak spot."

Her hand rose up. Her fingers curled over his pinky.

"Good. Now, if I were attacking, you would twist that digit back as hard as you can. If his grip eases on your waist because he's battling pain and surprise, you haul ass away, understand? The goal is to always get away."

"Yes." Her hand fell back down to her side.

"Next lesson." The scent of strawberries filled his nose. "Head, knees, and elbows. Those are the hardest parts of your body, and they are the ones that can cause fast, rough damage to an attacker. If the prick has you from behind and your hands aren't free, then slam your head back as hard as you can. You might break his nose. You might just hurt him like hell and that will make him loosen his grip. Like I said, the goal is always for you to get free. You can also take your elbow and shove it back." He pulled her elbow back, showing her exactly how to target her attack. "I know the attack at the museum happened fast, and there was little time to think. Don't worry about thinking. Just act. Just attack."

He went through drills with her, showing her again and again just how to get free of his holds. Her body still trembled, but she followed his directions perfectly.

"Attacks are often about balance," he told her. "Just because someone is bigger, it doesn't mean you can't take their ass down." He moved in front of her. "Front attack," Jake explained. "I'm coming at you, and your goal is to use my own momentum against me so that you can drop me to the floor."

"That's not going to work. There is no way I can drop you." She seemed definite.

"It will work." He was equally definite. "Lean away from the attack."

Biting her lower lip, she eased her upper body back.

"When I grab for you, you also grab for me. Get your hands on my arm or on my shirt and you *pull* me toward you and down."

She stared at him with her intense gaze.

"Reposition your leg. Slide it behind mine. That's going to help throw off my balance. You'll trip me." He showed her where to place her leg so that it was now behind his. "It's the unexpected that will work for you. You can get your attacker on the ground, and you can run."

She never took her gaze off him. "There is no way I'm getting you on the floor."

"Try it," he urged. She wouldn't believe it until it happened. So it had to happen. "You get me off-balance, then you get away. You haul ass and run." He pulled his hands back to his sides. Took a deep breath. Then he grabbed for her in a sudden lunge.

True's hands flew up. They curled around his arm. She yanked him toward her even as horror flashed on her face. Her leg hooked behind his. And he—

"Jake!"

He slammed down on the rug.

Immediately, she crouched beside him. Her hair fell forward as her hands pressed to his chest. "Are you okay?"

"Sweets." His chest ached. He lifted a hand and tucked a lock of hair behind her ear. "Didn't I say you were supposed to haul ass and run? Stopping to make sure your attacker is okay *isn't* part of the game plan."

She licked her lips. What could have been amazement filled her eyes. "I got you on the floor."

"Yeah, you did. And it was sexy as hell."

Her gaze darted over him, and then, shocking him—delighting him—True climbed on top of him. She straddled him, one knee going on either side of his body. "I didn't run because I don't want to get away, not from you."

Be careful what you say.

Her hands were still on his chest. He was still right under her. Like he wanted to get up. Hell, no. He wanted to stay exactly where they were. Though, it would be a bonus if their clothes were gone. And he was, oh, say...slamming home inside of her.

"What happens when the case is over?" True asked suddenly. Then she bit her lower lip. "I shouldn't have asked. Forget it."

He would forget nothing when it came to her. "Ice skating." A nod. "Though I should warn you, I can't skate for shit."

Her eyes widened. A quick laugh sputtered from her. Sweetest sound ever.

"Maybe we'll go out for some fancy dinners." He could not look away from her eyes. "Movies. A bit of dancing." Oh, yeah. Dancing would be great. Getting to hold her close? Sign him up. "I would imagine it would be the usual dating routine." Bullshit. There would be nothing usual about dating True.

"You—you want us to keep seeing each other?"

Now his stare sharpened on her. "You think I'm just fucking you and planning to walk away?"

"I think..." She pulled in a quick breath, then slowly released it. "I don't want to walk away from you. When I'm with you—despite the murder and the craziness that's happening in my life—I'm happy. Happier than I have been in a very long time." She leaned forward. He thought she was going to kiss him. He was more than ready to taste her.

True is happy with me.

If he had his way, he'd make sure she stayed happy every single day of her life.

But True didn't press her lips to his. Instead, her mouth went to his neck. A light, soft press of her lips. Then he felt the lick of her tongue against his skin. And...*fuck me,* the sexiest bite of her teeth.

His hands clamped around her hips. "True, don't play with me."

"I would never." Husky. Breathless. Designed to drive him wild.

She licked him again. Lightly sucked his skin. Her hips arched against him, and it was both heaven and hell. Heaven because she was riding his dick. With her legs curved on either side of him, she was in the absolute perfect position to rub against his aching arousal. But also hell because their clothes were still in the way. The clothes needed to go.

"I was rough last night," he gritted out.

"You were perfect last night," she corrected.

"Can you take me again?" He didn't want her to be too sore.

"Try to stop me."

Fuck, he could *love* this woman.

The thought stopped him cold.

No, no, it wasn't about whether he *could love.* His entire body had gone rock hard. *I do love this woman.*

True lifted up and frowned down at him in concern. "Jake? What's wrong?" Alarm flared on her face. "Don't you want me?"

"As long as I can breathe, I'll want you," he told her, dead honest.

Her lips began to curl.

He rolled her beneath him. A fast, quick roll. Then he was on top. Staring down at her and realizing she was far, far too important for any screw-ups. He had to tell her everything. No lies. No bullshit. "I'm not a hero."

Her long lashes fluttered. "Why would you say that?"

Because it was the truth. She deserved the full truth. He pulled in a deep breath. *Don't hate me.* But he had to confess. He stared in her eyes and said, "I took the case because I wanted you."

Chapter Thirteen

"Forget rocking around the Christmas tree. I'd rather just make love to True beneath it."
– Jake Hale

Her lips—red and lush—parted. "What?"

"I didn't know if you actually had a stalker. I just knew I wanted to be close to you. You painted me as a hero when I was just a selfish bastard, and you need to know the truth." His hands slammed down on either side of her body.

"You-you brought me home with you that first night because you *wanted* me?"

"You weren't staying in that low-rent motel. *It* was dangerous." An exhale. "But at that point, I had no clue if your story was real or not. I just knew you were a fantasy, and for the first time, I was close to you."

"Jake, I—"

Her words were interrupted because some jerk was pounding on his door. What. The. Hell? Now?

The pounding continued.

Her eyes were on him. He didn't want to move. He needed to—hell, Jake wasn't sure what he should do. Ask for forgiveness? Tell her that he was insanely in love with her? Would she even believe that? He'd just fully figured that shit out himself. She'd walked into his life less than what—forty-eight hours ago? Seventy-two? Who would believe love happened that fast?

It wasn't fast. I think part of me has been in love with her since we were sixteen. Since the first time I didn't have that damn, fancy-ass calculator for math class because the last thing I'd wanted to do was ask mom for more money. I was in the middle of the class, glaring around, and True shyly passed her calculator to me. She'd shared with him every day and never said a word about it.

So, yeah, he'd been falling in love with her for a very long time.

The pounding came again.

His jaw clenched. "Stay here." Because they'd set the trap for the perp. And though he seriously doubted the SOB would just show up and *knock* on the door, he didn't want to take chances with True's safety. Jake jumped to his feet. He marched for the front door, and as he did, he pulled his phone from his back pocket. A tap on the screen had him getting a view of his front porch via his doorbell camera.

And he could clearly see the jerk pounding away so hard. *Hell. Not what I need right now.*

Jake wrenched open the door. "What are you doing here?"

A perp wasn't at his door. His brother Tommy was.

Tommy frowned at him. "Uh, hello to you, too, brother dearest." He didn't wait to be invited inside. He just strode right over the threshold. Like he owned the place. He didn't. "And I'm here for our annual *we-hate-Christmas-so-let's-get-drunk-and-complain* celebration. I'm here because —" Tommy broke off. He pointed. "You have a Christmas tree in your den."

"Astute of you to notice."

But the tree wasn't the only thing Tommy had noticed.

True was on her feet. Standing beside the massive tree, she had her hands tucked behind her back.

"And you have...you have a *True* beneath your tree," Tommy loudly whispered. *Loud whisper, yep, that would be Tommy.* "Damn, bro." Tommy cut him a glance. "You must have been extremely good this year. I mean, to finally get that wish you've had for so long? Are you delirious right now? Hey, do you remember when I found that old photo of her that you used to carry in your wallet? I swear, you took that thing half-way around the world with you and—"

"*Thank you,* Tommy." That wasn't a whisper. But Jake's words were loud. Very, very loud. Loud enough to cut through his oversharing brother's ramble. "I do remember that, thank you. Thank you so much for bringing it up. Right in front of True." Jake cleared his throat. "Now, how about you just scoot on out, and I'll catch up with you tomorrow?"

But Tommy wasn't scooting anywhere. Well, actually, he was. He was scooting closer to True. Jake shut and locked the front door and followed his brother back to the den.

As he closed in on True, Tommy removed his black gloves and shoved them into the pocket of his billowing coat. Tommy was a clotheshorse. Probably because they'd grown up with secondhand items, Tommy now only bought the most expensive things he could find. Custom fits, most days. He was always ragging on Jake to up his style game, but it wasn't like you needed a fancy suit when you were running down bounties.

Tommy extended his hand to True. "Do you remember me?" he asked her. "I was two years behind you in school. Thomas Hale, at your service."

She took his hand. Gave it a quick shake. "I remember you. No one ever forgets the Hale brothers."

"Aw, right. Back in the day, we were the *Raising Hales,* weren't we?" A shake of his head at the old nickname. Yes, they had raised plenty of hell. So the nickname fit. "But we settled down since then," Tommy assured her. "Or at least, I have."

He hadn't let go of True's hand.

"You are even more beautiful now," Tommy murmured. "Has my brother told you that? He's not big on compliments, so he probably hasn't."

"True is fucking gorgeous. She always has been." Jake hauled his brother—and his brother's hand—away from True.

"How did you get True here?" Tommy squinted at him. "You always got tongue-tied around her in school. Do you remember how you used to just growl and—*hey! Stop!*"

He did not stop. In fact, Jake shoved his brother toward the front door even harder. "Time to go."

"But it's our annual *we-hate-Christmas—*"

"I don't hate it," Jake cut through his brother's words. "I don't hate it at all."

Tommy's stare darted back to True. "Yeah." Soft. "I guess you don't, not anymore." He pulled free of Jake's grip. "Gonna tell me how you worked this miracle? Because last I knew, you were just giving her stalkery looks when you saw her in the coffee shop."

Jake glowered. "You can stop oversharing at any point." Seriously, any point. Jake raked a hand over his face. "True is in danger."

That news wiped the smile off Tommy's face. "What?"

"She's been the victim of several attacks. A dead body was found in her house."

Tommy managed to shut his gaping mouth. "Are you serious?"

Did it look like he was joking? And why in the world would he ever joke about True's safety?

"I've been out of town—a ski trip with some colleagues to Vail. I had no idea..." Tommy shook his head. "So she's here because you're...what, protecting her? I don't get it. You're protecting her...with a giant Christmas tree?"

His brother was a pain in his ass. "She's staying with me because I'm keeping her safe."

"But you never put up a Christmas tree. Not since you moved out of mom's place when you were eighteen and you enlisted."

Tommy was fixated on the tree. "I put one up now." Or, rather, Perry had technically brought in the tree for him.

"You did it for her. Because she's...in danger?"

The floor creaked behind him. Jake knew True was closing in. "Because I want her happy. The tree makes her happy, so we have a tree." It was not a big deal.

Tommy's eyelids flickered. "Shit. This is gonna be bad, isn't it?"

Bad? Yeah. If True told him that he needed to get his sorry self out of her life, it would be bad. If she was furious because of what he'd done, it would be bad. And she had to be furious. Talk about your manipulative pricks—that was him.

"We'll have to start a new tradition, I guess," Tommy

announced after a thoughtful moment. "But that's cool. Just don't make me start singing carols. I will kick your ass if you try."

Tommy couldn't kick his ass on the best of his brother's days.

Tommy craned around Jake. "He's not a bad guy." Gruff. "Actually, he's the best guy I know. He paid for my college and law school. Saw more hell on earth than most people can imagine while he was doing his special ops work, but he never shares those nightmares with anyone. He never shares any pain with anyone. He also doesn't get a lot of joy."

Why, *why* did his brother have such a big mouth? Jake didn't talk enough. Tommy talked too freaking much.

"Can you give him some joy, True?" Tommy asked. "Or are you just here because he's keeping you safe?"

Wrong question to ask her. Jake unlocked and yanked open the front door. "See you tomorrow, Tommy."

"I thought it was a fair question. I mean, don't you want to know—"

He pushed his brother across the threshold and hauled the door closed behind them. "I'm trying to convince the woman to give me a chance." Low, meant just for Tommy. Though, considering his confession about why he'd taken her case, that chance had probably been blown to hell and back. "This is important. *She* is important."

Tommy nodded. "Important enough for a tree."

"Stop harping on the tree."

Tommy rubbed his jaw. "It's a pretty tree. Little bit lopsided. Could use some lights." His hand fell. "Maybe I'll even put one up at my place." A smile tugged at his lips. "Do you remember that year when I got the football that had been autographed by the University of Georgia quarterback? Thought that was like...the best thing in the world. I was eight and, I swear, I slept with that football for months after Christmas. I took it everywhere. Showed everyone." An exhale. "Thought Santa had some serious connections in order to get me that ball. He had to be a Georgia fan, right?"

Jake didn't say a word.

"I still have that football. Guy who signed it went on to be a legend in the NFL. Always thought that was the most amazing present ever." Tommy turned away. Took two steps. Stopped. "It took me years to realize that you'd given me that football."

Cold wind blew against Jake's face. Small snowflakes danced in the air around him.

"How'd you pull it off?" Tommy looked back at him. "How long did you stand in line to get me that autograph?"

It hadn't been a line. It had just been him, waiting hours and hours outside of the locker room at the University of Georgia. A scrawny kid who'd scraped and saved and taken the bus to the college. His mother had been furious when he finally came home. She'd thought that he'd run away.

"Don't know what you're talking about," Jake told his brother. "I need to get back inside." He turned away and reached for the doorknob.

"The football wasn't the best present I ever got. You were the best present."

Shit. "Don't you dare get all emotional on me."

"I would never."

Yeah, he would.

"Just...thanks for being my brother. That's all I'm saying."

Jake whipped around and stared in surprise at Tommy.

"If she's smart, she'll fall in love with you, and this will just be the first of many Christmases when I come over to find True and a giant Christmas tree waiting at your place. You deserve some happiness, brother. And I hope you get it." Tommy pulled out his gloves. "Damn cold out here. We're supposed to get a lot more snow soon. A white Christmas will be fun, don't you think?"

"It will be a pain in the ass." Automatic words. Words that he...didn't mean.

Tommy laughed. "Bah humbug, to you, too." He waved and darted for his car.

"Tommy!"

His brother glanced back.

Jake swallowed. Twice. "Merry Christmas."

A wide smile split Tommy's face. "Didn't kill you to say it, did it?" Laughing, he hurried away.

No, it hadn't killed him.

Jake swung away. He twisted the doorknob and headed inside. Silence waited for him. Squaring his shoulders, he strode for the den. He and True had to finish their talk. The one where he very much hoped she didn't tell him that they were done.

"True, I—"

He drew up to a dead stop.

True stood near the Christmas tree again. Only she wasn't alone. A man in a bulky, black coat—a man wearing a black ski mask over his face and gloves on his hands—stood right beside her. And in one of his glove-covered hands, he held a gun.

A gun that was pressed to True's head.

Every muscle in Jake's body locked down.

"Ho, ho, ho, bastard," the man in the mask rasped. "Don't make another move, or I will pull the trigger, and your big Christmas gift this year will be one dead True."

Chapter Fourteen

"I didn't need to be visited by three Christmas spirits. I just needed one to change my life.
Hello, Ghost of Christmas Past. Now that you're here, don't ever leave me."
– Jake Hale

("Yeah, also, I think old Ebenezer was technically visited by four spirits—doesn't Jacob Marley count as a spirit? And why the hell wasn't Scrooge scared straight as soon as he saw all those chains?")

He'd snuck in the back door. True had been so focused on Jake and his brother that she hadn't even realized the intruder had been in the condo, not until it was too late.

He'd had the gun on her, so she hadn't been able to risk calling out a warning to Jake. One of the jerk's hands held the gun, and the other gripped her left shoulder. His fingers curled around her, digging into her skin.

"Are you hurt, True?" Jake asked softly.

"No." Just angry. And scared. Correction, terrified.

"You shouldn't have come back to town, True," the man in the mask said as his fingers bit deeper into her. "Things were *fine.* No one cared about the old shit at the museum. I could pick up a few pieces whenever I wanted. Could take a few jewels from old necklaces or earrings and fence them. Who the hell was gonna know?"

"Dylan Dunn. He knew." Jake nodded. "Did he help you fence the stuff you took? Was he working with you?"

"That guy—all he had to do was *scare* True away. So freaking simple. She was going to start hauling all kinds of shit out in the new year. The thefts were bound to be found then! I had to do something—scaring her out of town seemed like the best plan." An angry exhale. "But the closer he got to True, the more Dylan started liking what he was doing. Too damn much. Liking *her.*"

He kept his voice a rasp, but it was still familiar to True. Her heart galloped in her chest as she stared at Jake. His face showed no emotion. But his eyes glittered with an absolutely lethal intent. She knew he was just waiting for the moment to attack.

She had to give him that moment.

First, though, the man in the mask needed to get the hell away from her. *Was he holding the same gun that had been used to shoot Dylan Dunn?*

"I did you a favor," the man beside her revealed. "He was waiting in that house for you. Dylan would have *hurt* you."

"You have a gun to my head," True pointed out in what she thought was a surprisingly steady voice. "Doesn't that mean you're going to hurt me, too?" Sure seemed that way to her.

He lifted the gun from her head. And pointed it at Jake. "I need the computer. Thought I'd taken care of that problem already when I smashed it, but then you whisked the parts out of the museum. You aren't fixing shit. I need the computer." A rush of air. An angry exhale. "True, get your boyfriend to turn it over, and I'll disappear."

The computer wasn't there. They couldn't turn over what they didn't have.

"It's in the bedroom," Jake said. "I'll go get it."

And he took a step forward. One, then another. Toward them. Not toward the bedroom.

Her captor barked out a laugh. "You think I'm an idiot? You'll just go for a gun if you head in the bedroom. And dammit, *stop! Stop or I will shoot!*"

Jake's gaze cut to hers. "Did you like the gift, sweets? The one I gave you tonight?"

He wasn't talking about the tree. She nodded. "Best gift ever." Her hand rose toward her left shoulder. Then, in a flash, she grabbed her captor's gloved pinky finger. She yanked it back and out and heard the snap with a savage satisfaction.

Her attacker screamed. Filled with growing fury, her elbow rammed back into him, as hard as she could ram it, and True leapt forward.

Jake grabbed her. Practically threw her across the room. "*Get out!*" he roared at True.

And he leapt for her attacker.

True whipped back around. She saw the gun come up as the masked man took aim at Jake. "*No!*" The scream tore from her as the world seemed to stop. The man in the mask was going to shoot at Jake. He was going to kill Jake.

No, no, no! "Braden!" True yelled the masked man's name. "*Don't!*"

His head whipped toward her. His hold on the gun seemed to loosen.

Jake ripped the gun from him. Slung it so it soared over the couch. Then Jake was grabbing the masked man—*it's Braden, I know it's Braden.* Even though he'd disguised his voice, she'd still recognized it.

Jake pummeled Braden. Swung his fist at the younger man over and over again. Braden tried to fight back, but his swipes were pitiful. True scrambled around the couch and picked up the gun. She clutched it with shaking fingers and took aim.

Just as she took aim, Jake swung out hard and hit Braden with such stunning force that the masked attacker slammed into the Christmas tree. The whole tree wobbled, then crashed to the floor, taking Braden down with it.

Braden let out a low groan. He didn't get up.

Jake grabbed the Christmas tree lights that were in a brown box near him. He looped the lights around their attacker's wrists. Then his feet. Jake bound him completely. When the intruder was secure, Jake grabbed the ski mask and ripped it off the other man's face.

Braden groaned again. Blood dripped from his busted lip. "B-bastard..."

"Hello, Braden," Jake snarled right back. "Made the naughty list this season did you, you sonofabitch?"

Braden twisted and heaved but couldn't get free of the lights.

"You've been stealing from the museum," True accused. She crept closer, but she did not lower the gun.

Braden's fuming glare shot to her. "Why the hell couldn't you just *leave?* I only wanted you to leave town.

No one had to get hurt! But you wouldn't get scared off, no matter what Dylan and I did. Then Dylan—shit, he got *crazy.* Or *crazier* because I knew the bastard was always a bit unhinged. I knew I had to be careful with him—knew it ever since I met him when I was doing psych research on rehabilitating criminals." A rough laugh tore from him. "It was so perfect at first. I took things that had been forgotten. Dylan sold them. We split the cash. But you came to town, you landed the Egyptian display, and you got all of those big ideas about revitalizing the museum. You were gonna ruin everything. Everything! *I just wanted you to leave!*" Spittle flew from his mouth.

"And I want her to stay, asshole," Jake blasted back. He hauled out his phone. Dialed, then put the phone to his ear. "Harris, if those patrol units of yours are close, get them to come in my condo. Why? Because I've got our criminal mastermind tied up in the Christmas tree." A pause. "Yeah, I said what I said...*tied up in the Christmas tree.*" His gaze had never left Braden. "The perp is Braden Wallace, one of the museum guards. Yeah, the psych student. True has his gun, and I have him."

She crept a bit closer to the bound man. "You trapped me in the sarcophagus."

Braden's breath heaved. "I wanted you scared. Why the hell didn't you leave? Why did you need to stay in this town so damn badly?"

Because it had been her home. Her happiest times had been in this town. Before Braden and his pal had started to terrorize her.

"No one else gave a shit about the museum." Braden let out a shriek when he couldn't get out of the lights. "Why did you?"

Jake stepped closer to her. His fingers curled around hers as she held the gun. "Mind if I take this?"

"Please do," she whispered.

He slid it from her fingers. His gaze swept over her face. "You okay?"

Okay? She'd been sure that her attacker—Braden—might pull the trigger at any moment. She'd been afraid to call out for Jake because she hadn't wanted him to run inside and get shot. She'd been terrified that Jake might die in front of her.

"True?"

"I'm not hurt." Not physically.

"It's over," Jake promised her, voice gruff. "This prick is about to go to jail. He won't ever hurt you again."

"I have jewels!" Braden cried out. "I have cash! I've been stashing it all—*I can give you money, mister!* So. Much. Money! Just let me go. I'll give you everything I have. Just let me go."

Jake shook his head as he focused back on Braden. "Trying to bribe me? Or *buy* me off?"

"Yes!" Braden screamed. He was covered in green needles from the tree.

"No deal. I'm not for sale." Jake's jaw clenched. "There isn't enough money in the world for me to ever let you go. Not after what you did to *her*."

Braden went still as Jake leaned over him.

"You made a fatal mistake," Jake told him. "You went after the woman I love."

True grabbed the edge of the couch as shock rolled through her.

"You don't terrorize the woman I love. You'll be paying for that a very long time. See, I know where you're going, Braden. I know the kind of people who will be waiting when you're convicted of murder. The worst and most dangerous bastards you'll ever meet. Some of those bastard actually owe me favors." His smile was ice cold. "Maybe I'll be calling in on those favors."

"Oh, God." Braden began shuddering. And maybe crying.

"You terrorized her. You put her in a *coffin*."

"I was just trying to scare her!"

"Now I'm putting your ass in a cell. And you *won't* be getting out anytime soon."

She could hear the wailing of approaching sirens.

"What was it that you said to me?" Jake never lowered his gun. "Ho, ho, ho, bastard."

* * *

"You're gonna need a new tree," Harris informed Jake as he swept a critical gaze over the mess that had once been Jake's Christmas tree.

Correction, True's tree. I wanted the tree for True. A True who was outside, talking to uniformed cops.

"I've got to say, the Christmas lights were a nice touch. Guessing you didn't have any handcuffs at the ready?"

"They were in my bedroom."

"Sure. And the Christmas lights were just right there, so...why not use them to secure the perp? Makes total sense to me."

Jake leaned to the left so he could see around Harris's body. He wanted to put his gaze on True.

"That guy was confessing left and right. *Begging* for a deal as he was hauled out," Harris added. "Criminals aren't usually so quick to confess. What in the world would make him want to do that?"

Me. I scared him to death. "Who knows?"

"Uh, huh." Harris rocked back on his heels. "His vehicle was hidden around the block. Uniforms searched it and found a big key ring—kinda looks like the one that Robert Moss is always hauling around at the museum. I'm thinking Braden made copies of any keys he needed—he must have swiped the originals from either Robert or True. And he helped himself to whatever he wanted in that place. No one knew about his thefts."

"Until True came along." Jake couldn't see her. He really needed to see her. He felt as if he couldn't pull in a deep enough breath until he saw her again. "Bastard had a gun on her."

"I'm pretty sure that will turn out to be the same gun he used to kill Dylan Dunn. Ballistics will let us know for sure."

Jake edged toward the front of his house. "He said Dylan went crazy. That he was after True."

"Yeah, that's what the perp was telling me, too. Trying to spin it like he *had* to shoot Dylan in order to protect True. Not sure I buy that story."

Jake didn't buy it, either. "Braden was probably trying to cover his own ass. When he stopped being able to control Dylan, the guy became a liability for him."

"A liability that Braden couldn't afford." Harris brushed off a green needle that had tried to cling to his jacket. "Robert told Braden that you had taken the computer. That you could fix it. Dude panicked and came here."

He'd *wanted* the perp to come after him. What he had never, ever wanted? *For a gun to be pointed at True.* "I made a mistake."

"Do tell."

"True was put in jeopardy because of me."

Harris hummed. "Sure about that? I thought you were the hero who saved the day."

True appeared in the doorway. Just as the first time she'd come to him, snowflakes were in the darkness of her hair. Jake pulled in a deep breath. Slowly exhaled. "She saved herself. Broke his pinky finger—"

"Actually, the EMTs said *two* of his fingers were broken. He also had bruised ribs, a shattered wrist, and a bloody nose." A delicate pause. "Is True responsible for all of his injuries? Because your bruised knuckles would say otherwise."

True's gaze collided with Jake's. He swallowed down the lump in his throat. "Braden pulled a gun on her. He had to learn that was something you never, ever should do."

"Important life lesson, totally understand." Harris edged a bit closer. "What's gonna happen now?" Low. His voice only carried to Jake. "Gonna get to live happily ever after with the woman of your dreams?"

If she'll have me.

Snowflakes blew in the open doorway.

"Hate to tell you, buddy," Harris said as he clapped a hand on Jake's shoulder. "But this place is gonna be a crime scene for a while. You should find a new place to stay."

Jake barely heard him. True was walking toward him. Her eyes were on his.

That creep had a gun on her. I came in and there was a gun on True, and I could feel my whole world shattering around me.

So, yeah, he loved her. Might as well get that right out in the open. The love he felt for her had nearly ripped him apart. He'd been so afraid. More afraid than he'd ever been on any battlefield in any place in the world.

True kept heading toward him.

He'd told her that he'd taken the case because he wanted her. Not because he was some noble hero. *If only. I wish I could be a hero for her.*

But he wasn't. He was just a rough bounty hunter. A former soldier who knew how to hunt and how to *hurt* and he wanted True more than he wanted breath.

She stopped right in front of him.

His very own Ghost of Christmas Past.

The woman he wanted to be his Christmas Present. His Christmas Future. His everything.

Her hand rose. Pressed over his heart. "Jake."

Was this the part where she told him it was over? That she was safe and that she didn't—

"I need you," she told him.

Words from a fantasy he'd had long ago. Maybe he was hallucinating. Dreaming. Because she was his dream. A life with True would be his dream.

"And I think that I'm in love with you," she added softly.

He shook his head.

She nodded.

Then True threw her arms around him. She hauled him down to her. And she kissed him.

No dream. No fantasy. True was the real deal. His arms wrapped around her, and he kissed her back with every bit of love and passion he had. Every. Single. Bit.

Sometimes, Christmas miracles could happen.

Even to a former Scrooge like him.

Epilogue - Number One

"I don't need a tree. I don't need decorations. I only need Jake. He's the only present I'll ever want." – True Blakely

"Yeah, sweets, that's nice of you to say, but where the hell do you want me to put this big-ass tree?"
– Jake Hale, new official fan of Christmas trees

THE BAD GUY HAD BEEN LOCKED AWAY. BRADEN Wallace wasn't going to be causing trouble for anyone else, not for a very long time. Perry had managed to retrieve the data on the battered hard drive, and True and Aliyah had been able to give the cops an inventory of all the items that were missing from the museum.

True was safe. She didn't have to fear what waited in the shadows. She didn't need to look over her shoulder any longer. A good thing because she was very, very much focused on the future.

With Jake.

Her ex-husband had sobered up and left town. He knew they were done. When she thought of Richard and how she'd felt about him, those emotions paled in comparison to how her body and heart just seemed to *belong* to Jake.

When the gun had swung toward him...when Braden had taken aim at him...

"True? You ready?"

I don't want to think about that time again. But in that one, terrible instant, she'd realized something very important.

She loved Jake Hale.

Jake stepped in front of her. Or, rather, glided. Very, very awkwardly.

She grabbed him before he could fall onto the ice. "You do not have to do this," True told him.

"I promised you an ice-skating date." He regained his balance. Mostly. "We are having an ice-skating date."

He'd rented out the entire rink for them. Brought wine. Strawberries. He'd confessed that he might have a slight strawberry addiction.

Christmas music played from the rink's speakers. Beautiful lights hung around the place. The whole thing kinda looked like something from a Hallmark movie.

Then Jake fell on his ass.

And he took her down with him.

She was laughing as she landed on top of him, and he laughed, too. His laughter was rich and deep, and it warmed her whole body from the inside, out. His hands were on her, she straddled him as he pressed against the ice, and True just had to say, "I love you."

Her words stopped his laughter. Jake shook his head. "Just because I said it...you don't have to give me the words. I know it's soon, I know it's—"

"*I* know that I love you. And you've only said the words once to me. Though, technically, I think you said them when you were talking to Braden."

"Bastard."

"Agreed." She waited. She also made no move to climb off him.

He stared up at her. "I love you."

That's what I wanted to hear. She kissed him. Quick. A dip of her tongue into his mouth. Then she rose to her feet, being very careful to keep the blades of her skates away from him. "If you can catch me, I'll give you a night you will never forget."

His gaze blazed. "True."

She helped him up. It was the least she could do. Then she let him go. "Catch me."

"Don't tease."

"I'm not teasing, it's a promise." She turned away from him, but she didn't rush off. What would be the point in that? True wanted to be caught.

A moment later, his arms closed around her. His warmth sank into her. "Got you."

Always.

She shifted position so that she could take his hand. They skated around the rink and the lights gleamed and the music played and...

"Merry Christmas, sweets," Jake told her.

She stopped skating. She turned in his arms. "Merry Christmas, Jake."

"How about we make a vow? No more murders at Christmas? No more life-or-death moments? Just...you. Me.

All the happiness we can stand." His lips curled into a half-smile.

The sexiest half-smile in the entire world. "I can stand a whole lot of happiness," True assured him. She curled her hands around his shoulders. "Especially when I'm with you."

* * *

"ARE YOU READY FOR YOUR PRESENT?" True called.

Jake was in bed, naked, and waiting for her. Hell, yes, he was ready. The woman basically had to *breathe,* and he was ready.

The cops had given him the all-clear to go back inside his condo. True had come with him. They'd gotten a new tree. One somewhere in between Charlie Brown size and the monster they'd had before. One they'd decorated together.

That decorating had been fun. In his mind, he could see them doing that routine every year. And maybe one day, they'd have kids to help them with the tree trimming bit. A little girl he held up so she could put the star on the top. A boy who raced around the tree to help them put the garland in place.

And I want them to love Christmas as much as their mother does.

"Jake?" True poked her head out of the bathroom. "You didn't say you were ready."

"Trust me, sweets, I can't get more ready for you."

She flashed her mega-watt smile at him. The one he felt driving right into his heart. Then she opened the bathroom door fully and stepped out to give him his present.

I was wrong. I can be more ready. Because he'd just leapt out of the bed and rushed for her.

True laughed as he lifted her into his arms. She wore the smallest, skimpiest bit of nothing panties he'd ever seen in his life. That—and a Santa hat. His dick could not wait to drive inside of her.

"The underwear is edible," she revealed as she brushed a kiss over his neck. "Want to guess what flavor?"

"I have *not* been good enough for this." No way.

"Strawberry." She lightly licked him.

Yeah, he was *done*.

He took her back to the bed. Lowered her onto the mattress and helped her get rid of the underwear. He shoved her legs apart and his mouth feasted on her. Licking and stroking. Kissing. Devouring.

"Jake!"

He freaking loved it when she screamed for him. He didn't stop with her first orgasm, though. After all, he did love strawberries.

And he loved eating her right up.

She twisted and heaved, and he enjoyed his favorite treat in the entire world and when neither of them could stand it for another moment, he sheathed his dick in a condom and drove straight into her straining core.

She clamped around him. Her nails sank into his arms.

He withdrew.

She arched against him and slammed up to meet him as he thrust back into her. Somewhere in the condo, Christmas music played.

He didn't care about the music.

Didn't care about anything but barreling toward the insane release that he knew waited for him. With the taste of True and strawberries on his tongue, he drove relentlessly toward his climax.

She came again for him, and the ripple of her inner muscles sent him over the edge. He erupted into her, and the orgasm was so powerful that he felt it in every cell of his body. It rocked through him. Consumed him. Pleasure swept them both away.

Merry Christmas to us.

Slowly, his lashes lifted. He stared down at True. Her breathing rushed out, red stained her cheeks, but she was smiling at him.

True Blakely. In his bed.

His.

Her smile flickered. "I've been meaning to ask...did you really carry an old picture of me around?"

He was still balls deep in her. "Sweets, I've carried you in my mind since you were sixteen years old." But, yeah, he'd carried an actual picture, too. One he'd cut out of the yearbook. A reminder to him that there were good things in the world. Good people. No matter how dark things had seemed...how dangerous the battles had become...

Good people were out there.

People worth protecting. People worth fighting for.

Her hand rose and pressed to his cheek. "Tomorrow is Christmas Day."

Yeah, it was. But he didn't need some jolly man in red to bring him anything. He already had everything in the world he could possibly want.

He wasn't the poor kid looking at others and hoping and dreaming any longer.

He was the man who had everything.

Every-damn-thing he needed. Wanted. Craved.

And, hell, if there was a real Santa out there...and not

just the spies who lined the streets like the cute kid had told him...

Thank you. You gave me more than I will ever deserve.

"Merry Christmas, Jake," True whispered.

"Merry Christmas, sweets." His head turned, and he brushed a kiss over her palm. "Merry Christmas."

Epilogue - Number Two

One More Word From Jake Hale...

Want a final thought from Jake Hale? Well, here you go...

Merry Christmas to all...and to all a fabulous damn night! Isn't that how it goes? Close enough? I think so. Hug your loved ones. Enjoy the season. Be merry. Be bright. Be whatever you want to be as long as you are happy. As for me...I'll be here with True. Eating Christmas cookies until I can't move. Singing way off key with my brother Tommy. And realizing that life is what we make it.

So make yours something special.

Ho, ho, ho.

P.S. Oh, and be sure to watch out for the Santa spies. According to my friend Taneisha, they are everywhere. They know when you've been nice and when you've been naughty. Though, I do have to say...being naughty is one helluva lot of fun.

Want to read another Cynthia Eden romance? If you love cold cases and hot romances, then don't miss CRUEL ICE.

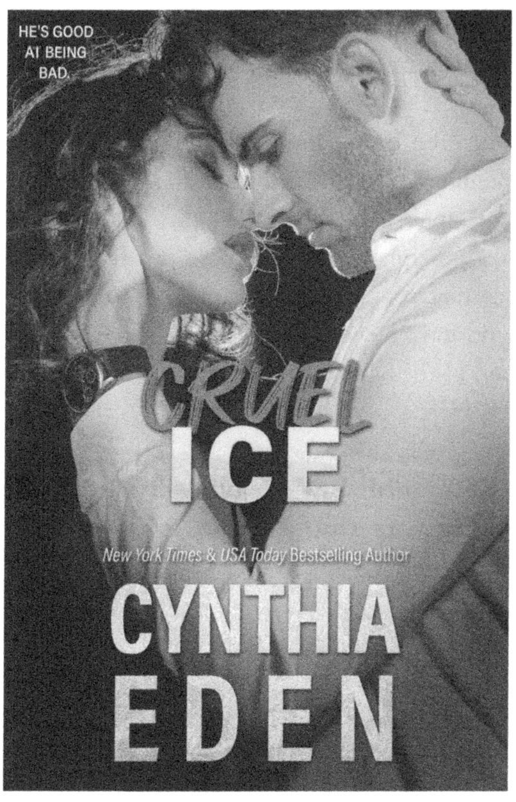

The sins of the father...are coming back to wreck his world.

Make no mistake, Declan Flynn is not a good man. He's never claimed to be. He's rich, powerful, dangerous...and, apparently, on someone's kill list. When he wakes up one night, tied to a chair in a dank basement, Declan is certainly less than pleased—and in a killing mood of his own. Then *she* appears. His most unlikely savior.

Marley Jones never expected to be the guardian angel to a man most people consider the devil.

But fate is often funny, and she's in the wrong place at the right time in order to save one very ungrateful and gorgeous billionaire. She's a low-rent PI, he's crime royalty (if you believe the gossip) and she may have just stumbled onto the first big case of her career. Now her job is to protect her new client—and in order to do that, she plans to stick to Declan like glue. He'd better get used to having her around. Intimately close.

First, he could have saved himself. Second, there is no way that Declan ever intends to let Marley go.

Good things—and people—don't come into Declan's life often. And when Marley inserts herself into what will obviously become one very bloody battle, the only thing he can do is protect her...even as Marley mistakenly thinks *she* is protecting him. By saving him, Marley put a target on her delicate back, and he intends to make sure that no one so much as touches a hair on her head. He also intends to claim the brave and fierce woman who calls to a dark and savage hunger that he's buried deep inside.

But an enemy wants vengeance, and he doesn't care about the collateral damage.

Someone wants Declan to suffer. To pay for the crimes his father committed. To unmask the predator who is now hunting both Declan and Marley, they will have to face the hell of Declan's past. Monsters aren't born. They're made. Declan was made into a monster long ago, and this beast will do anything to protect the angel that slipped into his world.

Try to take her from him? He will show you hell on earth.

Author's Note

Thank you so much for reading HOLDING OUT FOR A HOLIDAY HERO. I absolutely love Christmas romances—both writing them and reading them. They always make me feel extra festive. And it is such fun to curl in front of a glowing Christmas tree and get lost in a holiday tale.

I greatly appreciate you taking the time to read Jake and True's story. Our modern Scrooge needed to see that there was still magic in the world. If we look around, we can always find a bit of magic.

If you have time, please consider leaving a review for HOLDING OUT FOR A HOLIDAY HERO. Reviews help readers to discover new books—and authors are definitely grateful for them!

If you'd like to stay updated on my releases and sales, please join my newsletter list. Did I mention that when you sign up, you get a FREE Cynthia Eden book? Because you do!

By the way, I'm also active on social media. You can find me chatting away about books and life on Instagram and Facebook.

Again, thank you for reading HOLDING OUT FOR A HOLIDAY HERO. May your holiday season be filled with joy!

Best,

Cynthia Eden

cynthiaeden.com

More Books By Cynthia Eden

Protector & Defender Romance

- When He Protects

Ice Breaker Cold Case Romance

- Frozen In Ice (Book 1)
- Falling For The Ice Queen (Book 2)
- Ice Cold Saint (Book 3)
- Touched By Ice (Book 4)
- Trapped In Ice (Book 5)
- Forged From Ice (Book 6)
- Buried Under Ice (Book 7)
- Ice Cold Kiss (Book 8)
- Locked In Ice (Book 9)
- Savage Ice (Book 10)
- Brutal Ice (Book 11)

Wilde Ways

- Protecting Piper (Book 1)
- Guarding Gwen (Book 2)
- Before Ben (Book 3)

- The Heart You Break (Book 4)
- Fighting For Her (Book 5)
- Ghost Of A Chance (Book 6)
- Crossing The Line (Book 7)
- Counting On Cole (Book 8)
- Chase After Me (Book 9)
- Say I Do (Book 10)
- Roman Will Fall (Book 11)
- The One Who Got Away (Book 12)
- Pretend You Want Me (Book 13)
- Cross My Heart (Book 14)
- The Bodyguard Next Door (Book 15)
- Ex Marks The Perfect Spot (Book 16)
- The Thief Who Loved Me (Book 17)

The Fallen Series

- Angel Of Darkness (Book 1)
- Angel Betrayed (Book 2)
- Angel In Chains (Book 3)
- Avenging Angel (Book 4)

Wilde Ways: Gone Rogue

- How To Protect A Princess (Book 1)
- How To Heal A Heartbreak (Book 2)
- How To Con A Crime Boss (Book 3)

Night Watch Paranormal Romance

- Hunt Me Down (Book 1)
- Slay My Name (Book 2)
- Face Your Demon (Book 3)

Trouble For Hire

- No Escape From War (Book 1)

- Don't Play With Odin (Book 2)
- Jinx, You're It (Book 3)
- Remember Ramsey (Book 4)

Death and Moonlight Mystery

- Step Into My Web (Book 1)
- Save Me From The Dark (Book 2)

Phoenix Fury

- Hot Enough To Burn (Book 1)
- Slow Burn (Book 2)
- Burn It Down (Book 3)

Dark Sins

- Don't Trust A Killer (Book 1)
- Don't Love A Liar (Book 2)

Lazarus Rising

- Never Let Go (Book One)
- Keep Me Close (Book Two)
- Stay With Me (Book Three)
- Run To Me (Book Four)
- Lie Close To Me (Book Five)
- Hold On Tight (Book Six)

Bad Things

- The Devil In Disguise (Book 1)
- On The Prowl (Book 2)
- Undead Or Alive (Book 3)
- Broken Angel (Book 4)
- Heart Of Stone (Book 5)
- Tempted By Fate (Book 6)
- Wicked And Wild (Book 7)

- Saint Or Sinner (Book 8)

Bite Series

- Forbidden Bite (Bite Book 1)
- Mating Bite (Bite Book 2)

Blood and Moonlight Series

- Bite The Dust (Book 1)
- Better Off Undead (Book 2)
- Bitter Blood (Book 3)

Mine Series

- Mine To Take (Book 1)
- Mine To Keep (Book 2)
- Mine To Hold (Book 3)
- Mine To Crave (Book 4)
- Mine To Have (Book 5)
- Mine To Protect (Book 6)

Dark Obsession Series

- Watch Me (Book 1)
- Want Me (Book 2)
- Need Me (Book 3)
- Beware Of Me (Book 4)

Purgatory Series

- The Wolf Within (Book 1)
- Marked By The Vampire (Book 2)
- Charming The Beast (Book 3)
- Deal with the Devil (Book 4)

Bound Series

- Bound By Blood (Book 1)

- Bound In Darkness (Book 2)
- Bound In Sin (Book 3)
- Bound By The Night (Book 4)
- Bound in Death (Book 5)

Stand-Alone Romantic Suspense

- Waiting For Christmas
- Monster Without Mercy
- Kiss Me This Christmas
- It's A Wonderful Werewolf
- Never Cry Werewolf
- Immortal Danger
- Deck The Halls
- Come Back To Me
- Put A Spell On Me
- Never Gonna Happen
- One Hot Holiday
- Slay All Day
- Midnight Bite
- Secret Admirer
- Christmas With A Spy
- Femme Fatale
- Until Death
- Sinful Secrets
- First Taste of Darkness
- A Vampire's Christmas Carol

About the Author

Cynthia Eden loves romance books, chocolate, and going on semi-lazy adventures. She is a *New York Times*, *USA Today*, *Digital Book World*, and *IndieReader* best-seller. She writes romantic suspense, paranormal romance, and fun contemporary novels. You can find out more about her work at www.cynthiaeden.com.

If you want to stay updated on her new releases and books deals, be sure to join her newsletter group: cynthiaeden.com/newsletter. When new readers sign up for her newsletter, they are automatically given a free Cynthia Eden ebook.

Made in the USA
Coppell, TX
29 November 2024

41211911R00115